£1.50

THE H. L. MENCKEN
MURDER CASE

THE
H. L. MENCKEN
MURDER CASE

A LITERARY THRILLER

DON SWAIM

A Joan Kahn BOOK

ST. MARTIN'S PRESS · NEW YORK

Design by Janet Tingey

Library of Congress Cataloging-in-Publication Data

Swaim, Don.
    The H. L. Mencken murder case.

"A Joan Kahn book."
    1. Mencken, H. L. (Henry Louis), 1880–1956, in fiction, drama, poetry, etc.   I. Title.
PS3569.W218H18   1988   813'.54   88-11550
ISBN 0-312-02217-4

First Edition

10 9 8 7 6 5 4 3 2 1

FOR MARION AND
THE MEMORY OF HELEN

("... forgive some sinner and
wink your eye at some homely girl.")

1948

A good year for Harry S Truman. A bad year for Thomas E. Dewey. The conventions are broadcast for the first time on Philcos and Crosleys. Tallulah Bankhead is starring in *Private Lives*. The Hooper Poll lists "The Lux Radio Theater" as the number one radio show. Tojo is cross-examined at his war crimes trial. Hamburger is thirty-eight cents a pound. Rex Barney of the Dodgers pitches a no-hitter against the Giants. Cokes are a nickel. Cigarettes are respectable and almost everyone lights up. Banks pay 2 percent interest on savings. "Nature Boy" is the number one song.

The Fourth Avenue used-book dealers in Manhattan are in full swing. Uptown at auction, a copy of Poe's *Tamerlane* goes for $50,000. A suspected book thief and killer is on the loose. An impoverished secondhand book dealer named Howard suddenly has a windfall in the form of a rare manuscript. Reentering his life is an acerbic pudgy out-of-towner with slicked-down hair, red suspenders, and a cigar at the corner of his mouth, who has an affinity for *Huckleberry Finn*.

The years are numbered for the Fourth Avenue booksellers, but 1948 changes everything for Howard and the plump little guy from Baltimore.

ACKNOWLEDGMENTS

Among the books that were helpful in the creation of this work of fiction were: *A Mencken Chrestomathy* by H. L. Mencken, Knopf, 1949; *The Vintage Mencken* by H. L. Mencken, Vintage, 1955; *Minority Report* by H. L. Mencken, Knopf, 1956; *Prejudices: A Selection* by H. L. Mencken, Vintage, 1958; *Mencken's Last Campaign* by H. L. Mencken, New Republic Books, 1976; *The American Language* by H. L. Mencken, Knopf, 1963; *Supplement Two The American Language* by H. L. Mencken, Knopf, 1978; *Disturber of the Peace* by William Manchester, Collier, 1962; *The Irreverent Mr. Mencken* by Edgar Kemler, Little Brown, 1950; *Mencken* by Carl Bode, Southern Illinois Press, 1969; *Mencken: A Study of His Thought* by Charles Fecher, Knopf, 1978. Also: *The Life of General Charles Francois Dumouriez* by Charles Francois Dumouriez, 1789; *Papermaking: The History and Technique of an Ancient Craft* by Dard Hunter, Dover, 1978; *Great Forgers and Famous Fakes* by Charles Hamilton, Crown, 1980; *Collecting Rare Books for Pleasure and Profit* by Jack Matthews, Putnam, 1977; *A Primer of Book Collecting* by John Winterich and David Randall, Bell, 1966; and special thanks to Jack Biblo of Biblo Books, Brooklyn Heights, New York.

THE H. L. MENCKEN
MURDER CASE

1

"See that guy over there?"

Jacob Bluestein nudged his buddy Howard and pointed with a finger the shape of a quarter moon, the joints ballooned by arthritis. "Now him I don't like. I can look at a guy right away, without even talking to him, and know if I like him or I don't like him. And him I don't like. I'm not even sure I like you. Although your old man was okay, so I guess you got something going for you."

His finger was aimed at the plump little character with the Uncle Willie in the corner of his mouth, poking around the shabby books on the sagging shelves. Bluestein was gaunt and hunched with a hook in his nose and a stubbled chin to match.

"Say, I know that guy," Howard whispered. "He was a pal of my old man's. He used to come into the store a lot when Pop was alive. Those two would scream and shout at each other over everything. Politics to religion. Books to booze. I knew they liked each other even though they'd never admit it."

"Yeah, that guy comes into everybody's store," Bluestein said. "But he's a looker. Never buys. Always has something to sell. Just conned me into this Horatio Alger for a dime. I got another one on the cart outside the door. Didn't need no goddamned other one."

"You didn't have to buy it."

"So I bought it, I bought it! Him I don't like. Probably a goddamned Red."

Jacob shifted on his stool and bumped the crutch that was leaning against the counter. It slid to the floor with a crack, raising puffs of dust.

"Shit," said Bluestein.

"I'll get it," Howard said. "Don't put it so close to the aisle."

"Don't tell me what to do, smartass, or I'll take it and shove it where it don't belong."

Howard propped the crutch in an upright position. Bluestein had been threatening violence for so long that the guys on Fourth Avenue never paid attention. Just like they forgot where his leg had been. He had never bothered with an artificial limb. He kept the pants leg pinned to his thigh and hobbled around furiously like a madman on a crutch, which is what he was. He didn't talk much about his leg, other than to scream about the Germans in the kind of language that you wouldn't see in *Coronet*. But it was common knowledge that Bluestein lost the leg in World War I to a sniper firing from the roof of a farmhouse in the Argonne Forest. It was just after the Americans had captured the ruins of a place called Varennes. That was supposed to be where Louis the XVI and Marie Antoinette had been trapped while trying to run from the French Revolution. But Jacob Bluestein wasn't thinking much about Louis the XVI and Marie Antoinette while he was screaming in agony with dozens of other maimed doughboys in some bombed-out French church while a doctor hacked at his shattered leg.

Of course, Howard knew little or nothing about Varennes or Louis the XVI. Or the Argonne Forest. History wasn't one of his best subjects back in the Bronx at Evander Childs High School. And at the time Jacob was whipping the Hun, Howard was only eleven and too young to be thinking about anything but stickball and hot potatoes at 153rd and Melrose Avenue. A heart murmur, mature age, and a bad ear kept him out of World War II and he had the hearing aid to prove it. He didn't wear it much, though. He looked at lips if he really wanted to hear something. And most of the time, there wasn't much he wanted to hear.

"So who's running the place while you're loafing around Fourth Avenue doing nothing?" Bluestein asked.

"I'm not doing nothing," Howard said. "I'm here to see you. Besides, I'm about to head up to the library to meet you know who. And anyway, Lenny's watching the store."

"Library?" He snorted and bored at a nostril with a long-nailed little finger. "Your old man wouldn't like that girl up there."

"She ain't a girl. She's a mature lady. Besides, she's got great gams."

"Different, that's what she is. She's strange. Her mind's someplace else."

"She's preoccupied, Jacob. And why not? Ann's been working on her novel for more years than she wants to count."

"And that . . . that . . . Lenny! He's strange, too."

"Pop *would* approve of Lenny. I know for a fact."

"I ain't so sure."

"Lenny's helping me out a lot when he's not in class. I pay him."

"Don't see how you can afford to pay that loudmouth little prick on what you earn. That Lenny knows everything. Thinks he does."

"That's CCNY for you. He's studying history."

"You give these pimply, four-eyed little bastards a little education and they think they got wisdom."

"Lenny's not only going to City but he's taken up art. He's been going to the Student's Art League on Twenty-third Street to study calligraphy."

"Ca . . . what?"

"They call it calligraphy. Something to do with fancy handwriting."

"What the hell for? Lenny don't have enough to do?"

"You know Lenny. He's got some kinda fixation on beautiful books and manuscripts and stuff."

"What's he wanna do, move uptown and be like those hoity-toity Madison Avenue leather merchants? I tell you, sonny, too much learning only addles the brain."

Howard shrugged his shoulders. "Almost went to City myself, but Pop convinced me I wasn't college stuff," he said. "He used to say I fell out of my crib on my bean once too often."

"Shit, I liked your old man okay but he didn't know everything. You might have done all right up there at City. You shoulda tried. At least you shoulda graduated high school."

"I got all the knowledge I need. Right here. On Fourth Avenue."

"How would you know, sonny boy?" Bluestein said. "You never read a book in your life."

Jacob was right. And that was odd, because of his old man, Howard had spent his whole life around books. Pop bought and sold the things. He had a forty-five-dollar month-to-month lease on a storefront. Eighty and a half Fourth Avenue. Couple of blocks down from Union Square. Used books. The kind of property that shifted from hand to hand, owner to owner. Books nobody wanted and sold to guys like Pop and later to Howard when he took over the store. Some discarded book might be around the store for days or weeks or months or years and then all of a sudden someone would come along and take it and put it on his shelf and keep it there until he got tired of it or ran out of room or moved or died and then it would come back to Fourth Avenue, a little worse for wear but waiting for the next reader to take it home. The ones on the table outside the door cost a dime. A quarter or fifty cents for the ones inside. They were the better ones. Maybe seventy-five cents if they were clean and looked important and had dust jackets. Not much of a living all right. Nobody stood in line for books like they used to for cigarettes and booze and nylons and ration stamps just three years before during the Big One.

"Maybe I should have studied and learned more about things like truth and wisdom, whatever the hell they are," Howard would say to Brummell the Cat. "Maybe I should have taken up reading. But to me, it's not what's *inside* a book but what's *outside*, how it looks and feels. Ever notice that books are almost never the same?" he would ask as he dumped some dried cat food into the feline's bowl. Brummell was too smart to answer.

As Howard saw it, some books walked into the store dressed in cloth. Others came stripped down to their boards. Some strutted in in leather, their Sunday best. Economy versions showed up in paper. Once in a while one turned up in a case or a box, which proved that some fussy reader went to a lot of trouble to shield it from greasy hands and dusty air.

In fact, Howard saw books as kind of like people. Big, fat ones filled with lots of calories. Thin ones that weren't. Heavy ones weighed down by too many facts and figures, real yawners. Light ones picked up and blown away like feathers. Beautiful, handsome ones whose looks overwhelmed what was inside. Ugly, sinister ones doomed to rejection. Serious ones demanding attention. The battered and defeated, ready for retirement in those golden stacks upstairs. Winners, losers.

He never opened the damned things, except to shake them to scatter out the stuff that people would use to mark the place. Birthday cards, letters, party invitations, newspaper clippings, pressed flowers, canceled checks. Once a sawbuck floated out. Damned expensive bookmark. Worth more than the book.

Now Howard's pop wasn't an educated man, at least not formally educated. But he did read some. A lot actually. More than he let on. Everybody on Fourth Avenue saw him going through the tabloids cover to cover. He pored over the *Daily Telegraph,* marking the race horse columns with a chewed-up pencil. At least that's what it looked like he was doing. But sometimes he'd be caught reading something behind his *Telegraph,* something he'd keep covered up that he didn't want anyone to see, like a copy of Shakespeare's sonnets. He felt it didn't pay to impress anyone on Fourth Avenue with its seedy, wonderful books, even though he and his friend Butterman were known for playing hotly contested chess games in the back room.

Pop would bring home worn-out copies of the *National Geographic,* which a teenaged Howard would thumb through in the john, looking for pictures of native women in places like Borneo so he could see their boobs and maybe a tuft of hair down there at their cracks. Shit, they were ugly dumpy women with fat lips. But he'd hold the magazine with one hand and go at it with the other until his old lady would start banging on the door and rattling the knob and screaming for him to get the hell out. They didn't talk much about sex in those days except to say that doing it yourself drove you crazy, made you anemic, and gave you hair on the palms of your hands. Pop always promised he was going to tell Howard about the facts of life some day. He never got around to it. Howard's sex manual was *National Geographic.*

Pop just kind of tolerated Howard. He never told him right out he was dumb or anything but he always seemed to make it clear that he didn't think his son had a future anywhere but with him at 80½. After Ma died, Howard was all Pop had—except for Fourth Avenue. And Lenny.

Bluestein sold books too. Across the street from 80½. He and Howard were friendly competitors. Down there, the dealers all knew each other but they didn't help each other much. Bluestein, for example, had a policy. If a customer came into his store looking for a book and Bluestein didn't have it and he knew that Howard did, that was tough shit. He didn't help anyone. That never bothered Howard, though. Fourth Avenue booksellers were like that. Independent. If Bluestein didn't like the way a customer looked, he wouldn't sell him a bag of garbage, much less a book.

But all of the booksellers weren't as foul-tempered as Jacob Bluestein. For example, Peter Stammer, who ran a store at 65 Fourth Avenue, had in the middle of the room a coal stove on which he would warm tea to give to his customers.

After Pop retired, Howard took over the lease. Pop played gin rummy and drank Scotch for two months before a stroke got him while he was sitting in a deck chair on the veranda of the Cross Winds Hotel in Miami Beach, Florida. He died two days later. Howard drove down to the Cross Winds in his beat-up Nash to collect his old man's things, and they told him no one would sit in Pop's old deck chair anymore. It had been the third stroke someone had had in that same chair in a year. Pop was buried down there with his secrets and his guilt and the Shakespeare's sonnets he used to hide. He always wanted to stretch out in a warm climate. Funny, there was a freeze the month they put him in the ground. They lost their orange crop that year.

Pop barely made a dime on the store. He had managed to put only a few bucks away for his retirement. That, Social Security, and his gin rummy winnings kept him going until his stroke. There was just $298 entered in his bankbook when Howard went through his stuff. Like Pop, Howard was just breaking even. But the rent was cheap and he usually paid on time and when he didn't, Klein the landlord would come around to remind him that Pop always paid when he was supposed to and that he used to keep the place a little cleaner than Howard did. Anyway, the hours were his own and if he had a hangover or his hemorrhoids were killing him too much to open up and Lenny wasn't around, then he didn't open up.

The customers didn't care. They had plenty of choices. There were more than two dozen secondhand dealers, maybe more, on and around Fourth Avenue from Thirteenth Street to Astor Place. Like Dauber and Pine, Biblo and Tannen, Schulte's, the Strand, O'Malley's, Weiser's, Green's, the University Place Book Shop. There were five bookstores alone on Cooper Square in the building housing Cooper Union, where Abraham Lincoln delivered an eloquent speech before he was nominated as a presidential candidate. Folks came from all over to shop Fourth Avenue, buyers and browsers stepping from store to store. If they couldn't find it on Fourth Avenue, they couldn't find it.

Kind of an interesting street, Fourth Avenue, when you thought about it. Everyone had heard of Fifth and Third and the rest— but where the hell was Fourth? If you walked across Manhattan, there was a good chance you'd miss it because it was just a short stretch of blocks between Cooper Square and Union Square and ran at a kind of angle, like Broadway, not in line with Third or Fifth. Down at Cooper Union, it flowed into The Bowery. The tourist buses would rumble down The Bowery taking the sightseers to stare at the bums and the diamond mart and the lighting-fixture joints and the restaurant-supply houses. Howard could never figure out why the out-of-towners wanted to go gawk at the bums. Maybe they didn't have winos in Ohio or Illinois or Kansas. Up at Fourteenth Street at Union Square, just west of S. Klein's department store, Fourth Avenue merged into Park Avenue. Not the best section of Park, not where the swells lived, but still Park Avenue. Anyway, Fourth Avenue was kind of in between. Couldn't make up its mind what it wanted to be or to do except to maybe sell books.

"I tell you I don't like that guy," Bluestein muttered.

The plump little guy with the cigar ambled their way with a big Taft-for-President button on the lapel of his seersucker suit. Bob Taft was running in that convention year, but everyone said he was no match for Tom Dewey. But when Howard looked closer at the button, he saw that it had the year 1908, not 1948, under the word *President*. Come to think of it there was another Taft who ran for president in 1908, someone named William Howard.

"Help you?" Bluestein asked. Surly.

"*Huckleberry Finn,*" he said.

"What about him?"

"The book by Twain. I'm looking for an inexpensive reading copy."

"You see it back in fiction?"

"No."

"You don't see it, we don't got it. What you see is what we got."

"Quite so. Perhaps I assumed you had quietly hidden away a copy, waiting for some sinner like myself to ask for it."

The plump little guy took out a kitchen match from the pocket of his suit coat, scratched it along his rear end, and brought the flame to his Uncle Willie, restoking the cigar. The smoke orbited his face and his eyes blinked widely.

"Harry," Howard said. "Remember me?"

"Certainly," he said. "It's ah . . . ah . . ."

"Howard."

"Of course. You're on the wrong side of the street, aren't you? As I recall, your emporium is situated on the west side."

"Yeah, over at Eighty and a half. I'm just visiting."

"I, too, am just visiting. It usually takes a team of wild stallions to drag me to this cursed Sodom and Gomorrah. For many years I have easily resisted the temptation of living here. Business compels me to return to these tall buildings at shorter intervals than I would prefer. There was a day when I spent a good portion of each month in this overcrowded, oversized, unsanitary burg and except for periodic visits to Delmonico's or Luchow's or the Stork Club despised every waking moment of it."

Harry flipped some ashes from his cigar.

"New York may be the greatest city of the twentieth century but it has no more charm than a second-rate hotel or a circus tent," he said. "There is no distinguished thoroughfare and its parks are no better than cemetery lots. However, one of my few pleasures while on such visits was stopping by your father's bookstall. He was a most friendly enemy, a pigheaded man to be sure, but a worthy adversary who was much brighter than he let on. Yes, I do think about your father. For a book dealer he was a mostly civilized man. Even though he did favor a certain Herr Doktor R."

"He means Roosevelt," Howard told Bluestein. "What are you up to, Harry?" he asked. "In town for a show? A little Broadway? Some opera?"

It was a boffo season. That's what *The Daily News* was saying. Joe E. Brown was playing in *Harvey,* Tallulah Bankhead in *Private Lives,* and Henry Fonda in *Mister Roberts.*

"Hell no," said Harry. "Your theaters are nothing more than sweatshops. The seats are too narrow for malnourished Chinese and I can't stand being pinched and squeezed for hours. Breathing that fetid air. Sitting cheek to jowl with cads. Gaping at prancing imbeciles. As for opera, sir, that is to music what a whorehouse is to a cathedral. When you get to be my age, you'll learn that there are only two kinds of music. Bad music and German music."

"Don't talk to me about German music!" roared Jacob Bluestein, displaying his stump. "Goddamned Heinies. See that crutch over there? You can blame that on Kaiser Bill!"

Harry puffed at his cigar and half-closed his eyelids. "Your infirmity, sir, is the inevitable consequence of war. And war is always the result of political decisions that inevitably lead to personal tragedies such as yours. We should never have fought Germany in that war. England made the same mistake that we did by declaring against the Germans. If we had sided with the Kaiser, then Germany would not have emerged a bitter and dangerous rival. Europe would have been run like a Louisiana state-prison farm. We would have had a free hand in the Pacific and the Japs would have been docile. Our debtors would have repaid what they owe. And that tin-horn idiot with the shaving-brush mustache would not have materialized and there would have been no Second World War."

Jacob thumped his fist on the counter. "I was a corporal and I'm goddamned proud I served my country!"

"Soldiering, my dear storekeeper, is hardly a position of which to boast. Of all the arts developed by man, soldiering calls for the least intelligence and the least professional competency."

Howard thought Jacob Bluestein was going to have a stroke. His mouth worked furiously, spraying saliva, but no words would come.

"Every recorded battle," Harry said, "was nothing but a series of insane blunders and imbecilities on both sides. One wonders how any side could claim a victory. Even the greatest generals, Bonaparte for example, walked idiotically from trap to trap. Bunglers, numskulls, buffoons! Our so-called military heroes have proved as much ineptitude as second-rate lawyers or third-rate pedagogues."

Harry drew at his Uncle Willie.

"You, sir," he said to Jacob Bluestein, "were sent home maimed, dazed, and temporarily, at least, empty-headed. Like your comrades. And to what? After your days on the Western Front, how many of you contributed anything that was remotely interesting to civilization?" Harry shrugged. "I concede, however, that you are a cut above the rest. At least you stock your shelves with books for sale, although of course, too many of them are second-rate. Outside of an odd volume or two of Dreiser or Whitman or Conrad, of course."

Jacob Bluestein's chest heaved and his breath came from his mouth like steam.

"Now," said Harry, "since you cannot provide me with a copy of *Huckleberry Finn*, I must be off. I have a date with a Heineken and then I board a Pullman for a more cordial clime." With a flip of his wrist, Harry waddled out of the store. He didn't even say so long.

2

Jacob Bluestein was so riled, he couldn't speak for a good two and a half minutes. Then he reached under the counter and pulled out what was left of a fifth of Dewar's, same brand that Howard kept under his counter just like his old man had, and a couple of Dixie cups. He poured each of them a healthy shot. Bluestein drank his in a snap and splashed himself another.

"I told you I didn't like that guy," he said, as the whiskey began its mission of mercy. "I should have let him have it with the goddamned crutch."

Howard downed his Scotch. It was too early in the day but Jacob needed both Howard and the booze to help calm him down. The Scotch burned Howard's stomach and he wished he had a chaser.

Howard's old man hardly ever used big words but when he did, they were good ones. He used to call Harry an iconoclast. Howard had looked up the word once in a secondhand Funk and Wagnalls: a destroyer of institutions, someone who attacks established beliefs. To Howard, Harry was kind of like that Spanish guy Howard's mother used to read to him about when he was a kid, the one who was always charging at windmills. Only Harry would connect.

"Have another," Bluestein said. "To get you started to the library."

Howard waved him off. "Gotta scram, Jacob." Bluestein refilled his Dixie cup and turned to the crossword puzzle in the *Mirror* as Howard stepped into the noisy street. He headed up Fourth Avenue to Union Square, where he ducked into the subway next to May's department store and caught a number 6 IRT to Grand

Central. He got out in the shadow of the Commodore Hotel, where he stopped at a newsstand that was briskly selling the *Journal-American* and the *World-Telegram* and *PM* and the *Mirror,* with headlines about the Marshall Plan, the Berlin Blockade, and the new state of Israel. Guy next to him was humming "Nature Boy," and he began to hum it too, deep and low in his throat. He bought a package of Sen-Sen and then walked west to Forty-second and Fifth.

There were several police cars parked at odd angles in front of the library, as if the cops had arrived in a hurry. He went up the several tiers of steps, past the Corinthian columns protected by Patience and Fortitude, the lions. Engraved in the stone to the right of the bronze door were the words:

But above all things truth bearest away the victory

There were lots of serious-looking men in blue uniforms stalking the cavernous entrance room with its white marble stairs reaching upward on either side. By the time he got to the third floor, wheezing from the climb, he began to wonder what sort of mind would put the main reading room on the *top* floor instead of the *first*. His footsteps echoed as he entered the third-floor rotunda with its WPA murals on the walls and ceiling. Then he went through the catalog room, lined with cabinets containing thousands of narrow drawers for the card files, and into the two-block-long main reading room. It was divided in the middle by the delivery desk, which was more like a giant carved wooden cage where the books were picked up and returned.

Ann Elkin was behind the counter, stacking books into a cart. Howard leaned against a reading table for a couple of minutes to watch her. He liked her delicate features, made even more so by the faint laugh lines at the corners of her mouth. She wore her hair in bangs and that made her seem younger. She was wearing a flowered green suit with shoulder pads. By day she stacked books in the library. At night she chain-smoked and guzzled coffee in her Hell's Kitchen walk-up as she pounded out a novel on an old Smith-

Corona, watched by a testy canary that fluttered around protectively, except when the windows were open.

Andrea, the heroine of her novel, was a cross between the leading ladies of *Gone With the Wind* and *Forever Amber,* who plots against the tyranny of Alexander de' Medici in sixteenth-century Florentine Italy. Ann described Andrea as a "sexy, amorous beauty, headstrong and tenacious." She would read her manuscript to Howard for hours even though historical romances weren't exactly his cup of tea. Ann was worried that the sex scenes wouldn't pass the censor. But even if Macmillan had to water it down so that it wouldn't shock the pure and virtuous Catholics of Boston and their Protestant allies, Ann was sure it would explode as a best-seller. There would be excerpts in *Redbook.* It would be a Book-of-the-Month Club main selection. She might even sleep in a Pullman en route to Hollywood to have a hand in the movie version. Margaret Mitchell and Kathleen Winsor did it. Why not Ann Elkin?

"Where are your books on basket weaving?" Howard asked, leaning across the desk to kiss her cheek.

"Oh you," she said, kind of backing off, avoiding his lips. Her eyes were red and there were dark circles under them. Her skin didn't look healthy.

"Please!" she said. "Miss Hawksmith is around and she's very grumpy today because two of the girls called in sick." She sighed. Weary. "And keep your voice down. This *is* a library."

He spoke in a whisper. "You were up all night again."

"How did you guess?" A nerve began working, making her left eyelid flutter. "Christ, how I need a cigarette."

"When are you going to be finished with that tome?"

"I'm up to six hundred thirty manuscript pages now and I'm not halfway through."

"Didn't know there was that much to say about Italians. Let's go up to the Automat on Forty-second Street."

"Not today. We're shorthanded with those girls out, so Hawksmith is making me work right through."

"Tonight then. We'll meet at the passion pit. There's that new

Bob Hope movie at the Paramount. Stan Kenton's doing the stage with Julie Christie and Vic Damone."

"I can't. Smith and Corona await. And you know I detest Bob Hope."

"Smith and Corona may await but I can't."

"Be patient, you big palooka, I'm on a roll."

God knows she needed a roll. She had tried just about everything. After her father died spitting blood from black lung, she had demanded his old job at the Bolero coal mine in Cokeville, Pennsylvania. She was only a teenager at the time but her age didn't make any difference. She was told that women didn't go into the mines because only men were allowed to catch black lung. When her mother was fried to a crisp in a fire that destroyed their cottage, Ann Elkin went to Philadelphia and asked for work as a fire fighter. But the mayor decided that women were too fragile to lug hoses around. Then she met an alto-sax player who was hooked on morphine. He brought her to New York, where he played at the Embers. He was knifed to death by a pimp in a seedy hotel room in Times Square. She was angry enough to ask the NYPD to hire her as a street cop. The commissioner, clearly shocked, insisted that the streets were clearly too dangerous for women. Next she was roughed up by roustabouts on the Jersey City docks, where she had gone to sign up as a longshoreman. There was nothing open to her in the subway or the sewer, so she went to Hunter to study library science. Ann Elkin was her own woman and not unlike the heroine of her novel of Florentine Italy.

A couple of cops walked through the reading room in their double-breasted uniforms, studying the faces of the readers, scholars, loafers, and bums.

"What's going on?" Howard asked Ann Elkin. "Why all the law?"

"There's been another robbery. From the Bottom Collection."

"Bottom?"

"The rare-book collection. It's the foremost single collection of rare books in the country."

"Funny name."

"Dr. Matthew Bottom was a surgeon who spent his life collecting the rarest books in existence, mostly incunabula."

"Incu . . . what?"

"Howard, why aren't you wearing your hearing aid?"

"Makes me feel like an old man. Besides, who needs it?"

"Incunabula are old books."

"Old books? You mean I sell . . . whatever you just said?"

"Your books are old all right but not as old as the ones I'm talking about. Incunabula literally means from the cradle. Books printed before 1501."

"Jesus, bet they'd turn a few bucks. Just what did this guy steal?"

"I understand he made off with a copy of *The Canterbury Tales*. You know, by Chaucer. And a Euclid. When the curator caught him putting the books under his coat, he pulled a gun from a shoulder holster and fired a shot. I mean, we could hear it all over the library. The bullet didn't hit anyone but the man got away. With the books. The police thought he might still be in the building and sealed it off for a while, but apparently he escaped. Probably out the back into Bryant Park. The police have been all over the place. There have been several other thefts from the Bottom Collection and they think the same man did it. A professional book thief. And this time he almost killed someone!"

"They know what he looks like?"

"A pretty good description. Big man. Huge hands. More than six feet tall. Two hundred fifty pounds or more. Silver-gray hair. They think he's behind major library thefts all over the country."

"What's he do with those books?"

"He sells them. To unknowing libraries or unscrupulous collectors or dealers."

"Shit, he must do his homework. I wonder how he knows what's good and what's not and where to unload the loot."

"Well, whoever he is, he's obviously well-educated. Maybe a librarian or a collector himself. Or a dealer. He knows the books, knows the market."

The cops passed by them again on their way to the main corridor.

"Ann, I gotta change the subject," Howard said. "It's Lenny. He's getting on my nerves again."

"Keep your voice down!" she hissed. "Listen, Howard, you were the one who brought him into the store."

"Pop would have liked that," he said in his lowest voice. "You know that. He would have approved."

"Maybe."

"Lenny's got some sort of deal going. Something about a manuscript. Wants to get me involved."

"Whatever it is, it'll cost you money."

"But Pop would . . ."

"Pop! Pop! Howard, you can't go on trying to make up for all your father did or didn't do. His conscience was his own, not yours. You've got Lenny working in the store. You're practically paying for his college education. What more is he going to ask of you?"

He shrugged his shoulders.

Ann had an education, a college degree. Howard didn't. But they were drawn to each other since that day she walked into 80½ looking for books about Florentine Italy. His shelves weren't exactly bulging with books about Florentine Italy. She stayed for a Dixie cup filled with Dewar's.

Ann paled.

"Oh, oh," she said. "Here comes Hawksmith."

A skinny woman with a nose like a beak approached them, limping, one leg slightly shorter than the other, her lips moving as if practicing a lecture.

"I've got to get back to work. I can't afford to make the old bitch mad. I need this job until I finish the novel. Lunch tomorrow, maybe, if nobody's out. I'll meet you on Fourth Avenue at some bookstore."

"Which one?" he asked.

"Guess."

This time he managed to kiss her. On the cheek. She moved her lips away at the last second, averting his. An accident of timing, maybe, or her fear of the beak lady who was sweeping down on them.

Out in the marble corridor, he saw a double door with glass windows nearly opposite the main reading room marked BOTTOM COLLECTION. In the glass of one of the windows, shoulder-high, was a small hole with a spiderweb of cracks rising outward from it. He peeked through the shattered door and saw dozens of long glass-top cases lining the room, separating their pricey cargo from the temptation of human hands. But it seemed that the precautions failed to keep some of the treasures from the thief with the PhD.

He stopped a second for a sip of water at a marble drinking fountain, the spigot protruding from the mouth of an ornate carved brass lion, no doubt the offspring of Patience and Fortitude. As he walked down the winding stair through the lower lobby and onto Fifth Avenue, he found himself again humming "Nature Boy" and liking it because it was so sad.

3

"I'm telling you, Howard, it was one of the most cataclysmic social and political upheavals in the history of man, and we can have a slice of it." That was Lenny Gould between slices of roast beef on rye.

"Nix, Lenny. Ain't interested." Howard was eating the corn beef. Little more fatty than it should have been. But not too bad for a carryout from the Blarney Rock.

"Come up with me to the Newberry Gallery on Forty-ninth Street. Ronald Newberry will verify it. He'll tell you himself."

"Naw, Lenny, and stop chewing with your mouth open."

"Dammit, Howard, stop trying to be like an older brother. I want you to understand the importance of the French Revolution.

It meant the overthrow of the Bourbon monarchy and the creation of France's First Republic."

Howard sat on a stool on a raised platform at the front of the store so that even while sitting he could look down at the browsers and shoplifters. He was especially alert for the guys in the baggy coats who clustered near the *Esquire* magazines. Eighty and a half wasn't for the carriage trade.

"Yeah, I sell best-sellers all right," Howard would lecture Brummell the Cat. "But years after they drop off the list. You want something hot off the press, you go uptown to places like Brentano's and Scribner's and the Gotham. For rare, you go to swell joints like Duschnes and Kraus and Newberry and Fleming and Bartfield and the House of Books. Their books are for collectors. Used, secondhand. That's what I sell. My store's for browsing and my books are for reading!"

Brummell would spit. A gesture of affection.

Eighty and a half was a place customers came into wearing old clothes in order to dig under bibliographic piles, looking for the elusive item they could only find by luck. Howard had things organized, kind of, but in a store like his, there was always an overflow, books that couldn't join their neighbors on the shelves because there just wasn't enough room. Where did they all come from? You name it. Winos reeking of booze would stagger in with books they pulled from the trash. Kids with their mother's discards. Sons who stole from their fathers' libraries for a couple of bucks in beer money. An apartment superintendent with a carton of old books found in a dead lady's apartment. Once in a while someone would appear trying to peddle textbooks. Those he turned away. His old man found out a long time ago there was no market for textbooks, not for the guys on Fourth Avenue, which is why he put up a hand-lettered sign outside reading, NO TEXTS.

And magazines. All over the place were stacks of *Collier's, Coronet, The Smart Set, The American Mercury, Vanity Fair, Cartoon Digest, Vogue, White's Radio, Amazing Stories, Astounding, True Detective, Phantom Detective, The Saturday Evening Post, Liberty,*

Crack Detective, Air News, Argosy, American Astrology, Song Parade, Popular Science, and *Mechanix Illustrated.*

Some books were propped up in the window to give the folks passing by a taste of what was inside. Strangely, the books behind the glass stayed put year after year. Nobody bought them. That wasn't the case with the books on the card tables outside, the really cheap ones Howard would lay out when it wasn't raining or snowing. Some of the people who bought the cheapies seemed scared to death to actually go inside the store. Maybe they found it too uncomfortable to walk in, too intimidating. Perhaps that's why people joined the Literary Guild and Book-of-the-Month. They didn't have to actually go into a bookstore to get the book. No one had ever stolen a book from the display outside.

Eighty and a half Fourth Avenue was a long narrow room. Drooping pine shelves went floor to ceiling on either side. Down the middle were two waist-high tables with shelves underneath that ran the length of the store to the back wall where a washstand adorned with a can of Old Dutch Cleanser jutted into the room. A door marked PRIVATE swayed from its hinges to separate a tiny storage area so littered with books you had to walk on top of them to get in. The toilet was in a little closet hidden by a curtain. Every inch of space was covered by books except where you actually had to walk to get to the door or the john. Pop may have had it better organized than Howard at one time, before he got flooded by volumes that stayed around for years unsold. There were sections marked in crayon: HISTORY and PSYCHOLOGY and MILITARY, and so on. When the new books came in, Howard threw them in the vicinity of their category.

When Lenny wasn't around, Brummell the Cat kept Howard company, an especially mean-tempered and ugly feline with a strange knob on the left side of his head above his eye. Howard suspected that the cat had some sort of tumor. Brummell would frequently take a claw-swipe at him from his hiding place behind a pile of books. Just to let Howard know he was there and to put the book dealer on notice about who was boss. Brummell supplemented his diet of dried food by eating the cockroaches that thrived on either the pages of the books or the glue that held them together.

Pop had laid in a feather duster he had gotten up at Hearn's in the Bronx. But Howard managed to lose it. He spent half a day looking for it once, but it must have been buried under the books somewhere. So he gave up dusting. Anyway, dust was as much a part of the store as the sand at Coney Island. Klein the landlord would come in from time to time, look around, shake his head sadly, and mention something about fire insurance. Howard almost always paid the rent on time and Klein would almost always make sure the heat came on by December or January.

"Someday," Pop told Howard once as he stood with his arm around his son's shoulder looking at 80½ from the sidewalk, "this will be all yours." He was as proud as John D. Rockefeller standing in the Channel Gardens admiring the statue of Prometheus. Howard wanted to say, I'm not sure I want it, Pop. But he could never disappoint his old man. Inside, he guessed he always knew he'd become part of the store. Howard used to have a pretty good job running messages around William and Wall and Cedar and Pine to banks and brokers. Then he worked on the sanitation dock along the Hudson River, lining up the trucks that unloaded their garbage onto the barges that were towed to an ocean dump off the Jersey coast. The pay was good. But right after Pearl Harbor, it was even better at the Navy Yard, where he worked as a riveter alongside all those housewives from Brooklyn and Queens and Long Island. But 80½ and his old man kept calling him back.

"You ain't so bright," his old man told him once, "but I want you right here so I can train you the business."

"Pay attention, Howard." Lenny again. "Forty thousand people died during the Reign of Terror in the French Revolution. But it led to the words *Liberty, Equality, Fraternity.*"

"Say again, Lenny?"

" 'Liberty, Equality, Fraternity.' Dammit, Howard. Turn up that hearing aid."

"Liberty and so on, Lenny, they're just words."

"Words that personify the historical implications of the Revolution. If you can comprehend that, then you'll know the value of the manuscript I've been telling you about, a priceless document."

He dumped the scraps of his roast beef sandwich into an overflowing wastepaper can. Brummell leaped from nowhere to sniff around it. Lenny never gave up. Always pushed. Even as a little kid. Skinny. Thick horn-rims. Blind without them. Pimples. Lived with his ma on Second Avenue and 106th until she died. Now, there was something that Howard knew that Lenny didn't know. And that's why he had put up with Lenny as long as he had. His old man made him swear he'd never tell. And he hadn't. Except to Ann Elkin and he knew Pop wouldn't have minded about that.

Lenny's ma and Pop had something going for a while. A long while. That was back when Howard's own ma was still alive. He didn't know about the affair at the time, of course, and neither did she. Later Howard wondered why Pop was always bringing this ugly little kid Lenny around. Fact is, Howard didn't find out about the whole thing until after his ma died and Lenny's ma died and Lenny was left alone. By that time Lenny was old enough to take care of himself and he still came around a lot and when he did, Pop always got a little quiet and never said anything harsh no matter how annoying Lenny was. Which wasn't the way he treated Howard. Pop was always telling him to *clam up, for Christ's sake!*

It must have meant a lot to Pop for Lenny not to find out who his old man was and that someone was keeping an eye on the kid. That's why Howard gave Lenny work to do around the shop even though he couldn't afford it. Loaned him a few sawbucks and more from time to time. The money was supposed to be for college but they both knew they really weren't loans at all. Howard didn't expect to get anything back and Lenny didn't expect to return it.

Lenny may have been a smart kid but he wasn't smart enough to brush his teeth or clean his ears or change his underwear, which he had to do when his ma was alive. When he wasn't talking, which was most of the time, or picking at his pimples, he was buried in some book. Usually history. Mostly about the French Revolution. Half the time he was reading when he was supposed to be waiting on the goddamned customers. Or he was practicing that fancy lettering on art pads when he should have been putting books away. Jesus, he could get on Howard's nerves.

"Come on, Howard, go into this thing with me. It's a chance to cash in on history."

"You can't sell history, Lenny."

"Sure you can. Look at those shelves over there marked HISTORY. You're selling it. Now let's take it a step further. What if I were to tell you that instead of selling some battered-up history book, you could sell this manuscript for six, eight, maybe ten thousand dollars?"

Ten grand!

Howard turned up his hearing aid. That would be big-league dough for a small-time guy who sold nickel-and-dime books. Could keep Klein the landlord off his ass and pay the groceries for years. Could mean his ticket to Miami Beach. But he wasn't a Duschnes or Newberry or Fleming. They sold big-ticket stuff like that without batting an eye. Anyone without dark glasses and a white cane could see he wasn't in their class.

Ten g's!

"Lenny, why include me in this deal?"

"You know my situation, Howard. I'm a struggling student. I know the tuition is free but I've got to buy schoolbooks and I have other expenses. I just don't have the bucks."

"How much would this thing cost you're talking about?"

"Four tho . . ." Muffled word.

Howard turned up his hearing aid a little more. "Say again, Lenny. I don't hear you."

"Four thousand."

"*Dollars?*"

"Yeah."

Howard lifted a stack of books from the counter and dropped

them with a bang on the floor. Startled, Brummell jumped into the air and scooted under a table from which he turned and glowered.

"Now where the hell is a guy like me gonna scrape up four grand? Christ, Klein the landlord is coming around tomorrow to pick up the rent. That alone will wipe me out for the month."

"You can raise it, Howard! What about selling that old Nash you have? You never drive it. You could have a half-price sale on the books. That manuscript is the buy of a lifetime."

"And then what? I ain't the kind of guy who's going to sit around reading some rotting old papers. I gotta sell secondhand books."

"You sell the manuscript, Howard. *Sell it.* Just like you do books. Only to the upper crust. Collectors. Libraries. Museums. Universities. They'd die for it."

"And what do you get out it?"

"Twenty-five percent. When we dump it. Nothing till then."

Howard had a few hundred in the bank turning out 2 percent like clockwork. The '39 Nash he parked in Hoboken because stashing it in the sticks was a hell of a lot cheaper than in New York. He had some furniture and stuff and a few good pieces of jewelry his mom had before she died. Pop never gave her much. None of the old man's money was left. Most of it went for his funeral. First National might stand him for a loan. He might be able to hit old man Butterman who ran a funeral home on Amsterdam Avenue. Butterman and Howard's old man were chess pals. Howard would probably come pretty close to putting four grand together, but it would be the biggest investment of his life.

Howard remembered how his old man and Harry would argue about poverty and wealth, with Harry happily goading Pop into a rage.

"Problem with you, Harry," Pop roared, "is that you've never been poor, really poor, so you don't have no compassion for those without. There is a certain nobility about poverty."

"Nobility in being poverty-stricken?" Harry replied. "My dear bookseller, poverty may be an inescapable misfortune but it is no more honorable than a cleft palate or a cauliflower ear."

"What's more, Harry, a poor man grows from the experience. A painter in his garret, a starving poet. From suffering comes great art."

"A romantic superstition, my dear sir," Harry said, removing an Uncle Willie from a breast pocket, biting off the stem, and lighting up. "The artist cannot do his best work while starving. Neither can the philosopher nor the scientist. The best art is created by men who are well-fed, comfortable, and have peace of mind, not by those who are hungry, ragged, desperate."

"Dammit, it's not possible for everyone in this country to be happy and well-fed, Harry. Look around you! See the bread lines and the soup kitchens. The ragged women selling apples on the street corners. We're in the middle of a depression. Millions of our people are trapped."

"I do not take that point of view, sir. We are, indeed, a commonwealth of morons, but any person with modest intelligence and resolution can cadge enough money to make life soft for himself. What with average luck, it's absurdly easy to make a buck in this country."

"Then why the hell are so many of us starving?"

"The fact is, my biblio comrade, that America is a nation populated by third-raters. Not only are they standing in line for free soup, they are in full control of the state. America was not settled by the hardy adventurers of our imagination but by congenital dunderheads who couldn't get along where they came from. The people who reside here today are the descendants of those incompetents. The newspaper editorialists who, on the Fourth of July, compose nonsense about a great people in a great land are really referring to boobs. Scratch an average American and you'll find a Methodist under his skin."

"By God, Harry, you're full of shit! My father came here from Russia because of persecution by the Czar. We live in a land of immigrants who sailed here not just because there was something lacking in their homelands but because America was the greatest nation on earth. And those are the people who helped to spread art and culture and science to this country."

Harry blew his smoke into Pop's face. "In that last respect, I cannot disagree. In fact, there would be no intelligent life in the United States at all were it not for the steady importation of ideas from Europe, most particularly England. The average Anglo-Saxon American is in reality nothing more than a second-rate Englishman. The Italians have brought as much of the essential culture of Italy as a shipload of cattle. The Germans are on the cultural level of sausage makers. The Irish have provided nothing more than tap-rooms and crooked cops. And the Jews, they change their names to Thompson, Berkley, and Nelson in order to qualify as true Americans.

"Goddammit, Harry," shouted Pop, reaching under the counter for the Dewar's, "if you hate it here so much, why do you stick around?"

"Why do people visit zoos?"

Howard felt a hand on his shoulder. It was Lenny, shaking him. "Snap out of it, Howard. What do you say?"

"About the—"

"Yeah, the manuscript. We gotta move on it."

"Where is this manuscript, Lenny? Who owns it?"

"You won't believe this, Howard." He adjusted his glasses. His eyes looked like footballs behind his thick lenses. "It belongs to this old woman on Riverside Drive and One hundreth Street. She lives all alone and she's practically senile. She's had this manuscript for years. It was once her grandfather's. He was a collector. Now I happen to know she needs the dough because she might be going into a nursing home. She doesn't have long to live. She has some idea the manuscript is valuable but she doesn't know how valuable. If *we* don't grab it, someone else will. Someone who's not as honest as we are."

"Lenny, you sure that thing's not stolen? There was this robbery at the library this week."

"Howard, I'm shocked. On my mother's grave, so help me. Have

I ever lied to you, taken advantage of you? How could you think such a thing?"

Lenny was wearing Howard down. When he shut his eyes, he could see dollar signs behind the lids.

"What's this manuscript all about?" he asked.

"That's what I've been trying to tell you. It's called *An Englishman's Account of the Revolution of 1789 and the Taking of the Bastille,* by William Trevor Coxe. I tell you, it's a priceless piece of history."

"Not priceless, Lenny. Ten grand's worth of history. That's ten grand if we *sell* it. And if that old lady don't know how much it's worth, how come you're offering her four g's?"

"Can't cheat her, Howard. Honesty goes hand in hand in the book trade. And don't forget, we'll make twice as much as we paid for it."

"Let me give it some thought."

"We're running out of time, Howard. If we don't move now, we'll lose it. Listen, lock up the shop and come with me to the Newberry Gallery. Ronald Newberry knows all about manuscripts. He'll tell you how important it is."

"How do you happen to know a swell like Newberry?"

"I met him when I was working up at the Caesar Auction Galleries on Madison Avenue. You know, cleaning up and things. He'd come in for these big book and manuscript auctions. Of course, I knew his reputation, so I'd do things for him, run little errands, you know, stuff like that."

"So why doesn't your friend Newberry buy it?"

"That's the thing. He would if he knew about it. But he'll sure as hell find out if the old lady makes a move to sell it to anyone other than us. It's a small industry. Word gets around fast in the book business about what's come on and off the market. The news spreads, then it's curtains for us. We've lost our chance."

"Lenny, it better not be stolen."

"Howard, would I . . . have I ever? You've known me all my life. . . . How could you . . ."

4

He poured a cup of milk for Brummell, patted his tumor, and dodged the swipe of his claw. That was Brummell's way of saying love. The CLOSED sign was slapped on the door and Howard headed up Fifth Avenue with Lenny on the top deck of a double-decker bus. Someone was humming "Nature Boy" and that made Howard hum along. They passed B. Altman's, W & J Sloan, Lord and Taylor, Woolworth's, Kresge's, and Patience and Fortitude outside the library, where Howard waved instinctively, knowing Ann Elkin was stacking books inside. They got off at Forty-ninth. The Newberry Gallery was just off Fifth, east side, nestled on the ground floor of a fancy terra-cotta office tower. Howard knew that Ronald Newberry must have paid a fortune for those premises and that meant he had to earn one.

Everyone in books had heard of Newberry. He was always the big spender at the most important auctions. There were write-ups in *The Times,* the *Mirror,* and the *Daily News.* His clients were great libraries and universities and private collectors who didn't give a damn how much they paid for a bauble of history, the kind of folks Howard might be dealing with if that manuscript thing went through. Displayed in the front window of the Newberry Gallery were neatly arranged copies of a book Newberry had written himself: *Collecting the Rare and the Beautiful.* Howard thought that if he ever got around to it, maybe one day he'd write his own book, *Collecting the Common and the Ugly,* and display it in the window of 80½. A bell chimed as they opened the door to the gallery.

It was supposed to be a goddamned bookstore and they called it a gallery. Their feet sank into the carpet, wall to wall. For a book emporium, it was conspicuous for its lack of clutter. A few impressive volumes upright on dark mahogany shelves, others flat on polished tables as if waiting to be opened but probably never would. There was a sofa. Leather. And several French chairs. The place looked like a reading room. There was a speaker somewhere because they could hear some classical music, probably WQXR. At the rear was a carved oak desk with Queen Anne legs and behind it, a woman with legs to match in a tailored business suit. She looked up and with her hand flicked some imaginary lint off her padded left shoulder.

"I am Miss Kelly, Mr. Newberry's assistant. May I help you?"

Howard became aware that his tie was crooked and one of the pockets of his tweed jacket was pushed inside out. He stuffed it back in.

"Uh, Mr. Newberry, please?" Lenny asked, making it sound a bit like a plea.

"And who should I say would like to see him?"

"Uh, he knows me. Lenny. Lenny Gould."

"I'll see if he's in. You may . . ." she paused a little as if regretting what she was about to offer ". . . have a seat." She disappeared into a back room.

Lenny sat on the sofa. Howard stood nearby, running his hand over the leather.

"Will you look at this place?" he said to Lenny. "Wonder if they let people browse?" There was a large red morocco portfolio flat on a table and he opened it. "Look at this. It's some sort of manuscript. Wonder if it's like the one we're interested in?" The large sheets of paper were yellowish but smooth, not at all brittle like an old newspaper, the lettering in ornate script with flourishing letters that sprawled across the pages. It would have taken too much concentration to try to read it, so he didn't, but he leafed through the pages.

"Jesus, I wouldn't touch it, Howard. You know that if Newberry has it, it's got to be worth a fortune and you don't want to be responsible—"

"Quite right," said a voice behind them. "And, indeed, I would appreciate it if you would not touch it. It has withstood the ravages of the ages but it is vulnerable to a greasy hand of the twentieth century."

He was a tall man with gray hair and a thin mustache, dressed in a dark double-breasted suit. He might have been handsome had it not been for an eye that did not track, so that no one was sure which eye he was looking into. A huge gold ring weighed down his left pinkie. Lenny jumped up.

"Mr. Newberry, this is my friend Howard I told you about. He's a dealer, too. Runs his own place down on Fourth Avenue."

"Mr. Howard . . ." Newberry said.

"No, no. Howard's my fir—"

"I've been meaning to get down to Fourth Avenue," Newberry said, "but I never seem to have the time. Slumming is such a lark." He smiled to show he was just being friendly. "No offense."

The Fourth Avenue bookman started to put out his hand but Newberry kept his arms to their sides, so Howard dropped his wrist, feeling foolish. Newberry pulled a long cigarette from a gold case and lit it with a gleaming lighter. Howard thought he had seen cigarettes like that before. Foreign. Gauloise, someone had said. Howard smoked Chesterfields, himself. The doctors said they were better for your health than those foreign brands.

"The manuscript you were looking at on the table," Newberry said, exhaling fumes. "It was written by George Washington at Mount Vernon in October 1786, and is a ten-page account of his expedition with General Braddock in the French and Indian Wars. As you can see, it is unedited and has many emendations."

"Emendations?"

"Look it up. Fortunately, I have a buyer, albeit an anonymous one. I don't mind revealing that my client is paying one hundred thousand dollars."

Howard's mouth dropped. "I would have thought anything Washington wrote himself would be in a museum or something."

"There are many private collectors who treasure owning portions of our political and literary history. Are you familiar with *Tamerlane*? Of course, you aren't. It was published in Boston in 1827, a small volume of verse by someone who identified himself only as 'a Bostonian.' The preface tells us the poems were composed when the author had not completed his fourteenth year. Surely you know of whom I am speaking."

"Surely."

"There are only a dozen copies known to exist, outside of the one that I sold last year at a bargain price. Fifty thousand dollars. Surely, that's a steal for the first book by Edgar Allen Poe."

"A steal."

"I did have a First Folio. Shakespeare. But I'm unlikely to duplicate that feat. There is a good possibility I will acquire *The Canterbury Tales,* significant because it was the work of England's first printer, William Caxton. 1478. The copy, I understand, is defective, lacking twenty-seven leaves."

"Leaves?"

"Pages, Mr. Howard."

"Oh yeah, I knew that."

"But let me show you some examples I have on the premises, not samples of early printing, of course, but manuscripts." He led them to another table where he opened a green portfolio. "This is Washington's address to Congress defending his military invasion of Pennsylvania to quell the Whiskey Rebellion. November 1794. Signed and corrected throughout in the hand of the Father of our Country."

"What would something like that bring in?"

"I'm asking for sixty-five thousand dollars. Small potatoes for a *real* collector. And over here." Newberry opened another portfolio. "An amusing item. Washington was a mere lad of twenty-two when on December 17, 1754, he signed the original lease to his plantation in Virginia, Mount Vernon. That should fetch a mere thirty-five thousand dollars."

"How do you know these aren't fakes or forgeries?"

"My dear sir, we are experts in this field. Our merchandise is guaranteed to be authentic. Our reputation is impeccable."

"See, Howard, see." Lenny pulled at the cuff of Howard's jacket. "Manuscripts are big business."

"Too big for us. We're Fourth Avenue small fry."

"Not too big," Lenny said. "Maybe thirty-five thousand dollars is out of our league but not . . . not . . ."

"Not what, young man?" Newberry asked, deeply inhaling his cigarette.

"Uh, Mr. Newberry, I came in because I wanted you to, wanted you to tell my friend here about this manuscript I mentioned to you before. You know, the one by William Trevor Coxe about the fall of the Bastille."

"Certainly I've heard of it. *Everyone's* heard of it. But it's been missing for years. It has always been in private hands. I believe the last person known to have owned it was an industrialist by the name of Whitten. But the Whitten family seems to have passed out of sight, along with the manuscript. No one knows whether it was lost or stolen or just quietly tucked away in somebody's collection. It's not on a par with a Washington, of course, or that by any other major head of state for that matter. But my guess is it would demand six, maybe eight thousand. More if the *right* party was found. *And* if it is in fine condition. So, you know where this document is, of course?"

"I didn't say that, Mr. Newberry," Lenny said. "It's just that I've heard about it and I wanted my friend here to . . . to . . ."

"Come, Lenny. You're not going to fool an old trader like myself. I had my eye on you during those auctions on Madison Avenue." Howard wondered which eye it was since he wasn't sure which Newberry was using. "Certainly you know of its whereabouts. How much are you asking for it?"

"Well . . ."

"Lenny," Howard said, "we'd better talk about this."

"Do you gentlemen have the funds to purchase such a document?" No response. "I would doubt it, indeed. I can be extremely generous in my finder's fees should I acquire this item."

"We'd better go, Lenny," Howard said.

"You realize, Mr. Howard, that the British Museum has been

searching for the Coxe manuscript for a hundred years; that it would complete an irreplaceable collection of documents on the French Revolution composed by Englishmen?"

Lenny said, "Yeah, I—"

"Shut up, Lenny," Howard said. "Mr. Newberry, thanks for your time. You've given us a lot of information, helped us a lot. We were really just curious."

"Don't be foolish gentlemen. I have the resources and the contacts to make such a purchase plausible. After all, how many First Folios or *Tamerlane*s or Washington manuscripts or Chaucers come along? A livelihood is not based on the dramatic alone, although because of its elusive aspects, the Coxe manuscript would be dramatic enough. Come back to see me after you've talked it over."

Newberry again drew on his cigarette. One eye looked at Howard and then he turned his head slightly and the other eye had a look. He smiled. Miss Kelly with the Queen Anne legs came into the room and she smiled, too. The light bounced off an earring and then off of Newberry's pinkie ring, sending a blinding light into Howard's eyes. They stood by the desk, smug, surrounded by their rarities, eager to trade them, not to prize them.

"Until next time, Mr. Howard."

"Howard's my fir—"

"So long, Mr. Newberry," Lenny said.

Lenny and Howard left with the chime of the doorbell in their ears. They stood outside looking through the spotless glass of the window, inspecting the cover of Newberry's vanity book.

"Well, Lenny," Howard said. "Let's go slumming. It's such a lark."

5

"I'd like to sell this. How much for it?"

It was Pop's old pal. He had come in quietly through the front door while Howard was sitting behind the counter poring over the *Daily News*.

"Harry! Knew you'd be back."

"Alas, commerce has compelled my return to your garbage-strewn streets. Will you purchase this book or take it in trade?"

The book he was holding looked kind of familiar to Howard. Something by O. Henry, a reprint of *Cabbages and Kings*. He knew he had a copy that had been gathering dust for years in the bin outside the door. But, what the hell. There was always a chance someone would come along and take it if he waited long enough.

"A nickel," he said.

"Sold."

He hit the cash register and flipped Harry a coin. Howard plopped the book onto the counter, stirring a little cloud of dust.

"Wretched book," Harry said. "That fellow O. Henry was nothing but a cheese monger. He thought he was clever with his trick endings. But he was really about as smart as a smoke room and variety show."

What did Howard care how good or bad it was. He didn't have to read them. Just had to sell them.

"Conrad, now. Reading that man is like being caressed by Schubert, tutored by Beethoven—if a parallel can be found in music. An underrated man, that Mr. Conrad. When I think that the Nobel Prize has gone to such third-raters as Benavente and Heidenstam, while Conrad has been overlooked, why the judges who meet in Stockholm show they're nothing more than actors in a farce. There is no genius on this earth if Mr. Conrad was not a genius."

The only Conrad that Howard had ever heard of was this German kid named Conrad Sackel who used to deliver the laundry for his old man up in the Morrisania section. Tough son of a bitch. Put another kid's eye out with a bicycle chain once and never thought twice about it.

"I'm going to browse in your section on politics, this being an election year. A colorful cast of characters we have before us it seems—and in Philadelphia no less. Patriotic outpourings such as political conventions fascinate me. Even though they're all alike. All bla-a-ah! Stassen, Dewey, Taft, Truman, Wallace, Thurmond, Norman Thomas. A mangy crew of crackers, Ku Kluxers, and communists if I ever saw one. No doubt this Truman fellow will win. That's because the voters are boobs who throw their hats at the candidate most resembling their collective I.Q.s."

In fact, when the polls closed in the presidential election in New York City that year, 2,510,706 voters had cast their ballots. More than 3 million votes were cast that same year to elect Miss Rheingold.

Harry had his way with words but so did Pop and neither of them would come down until the book dealer sloshed some Dewars into a pair of paper cups, tossed back a couple, and joined Harry in cursing the days of Prohibition. Religion, politics, music, even dogs would have them screaming at each other. Yes, even dogs. Harry hated them. He even sued his neighbor once over some cocker spaniel that barked all night. Pop loved dalmations. Booze was the only thing Harry and Pop ever agreed on. How Harry would bitch about the Eighteenth Amendment!

"Thirteen awful years," he said. "For twelve years, ten months, and nineteen days the yokels had their way. The Great Experiment caused more suffering than the bubonic plague, the Thirty Years War, or The Ten Days that Shook the World combined. In fact, the alcoholic beverage is the greatest of all human inventions, better by far than heaven, hell, the radio, or even penicillin."

After a couple of drinks and a wave good-bye, Harry would disappear for a couple of weeks and then show up to start all over again with Pop, usually with a book in hand to sell.

Howard had heard that Harry was some sort of expert on language. He knew Harry used to edit a highbrow magazine and write books. Pop used to sell some of them. A professor, Howard guessed, from somewhere on the other side of the Hudson, Philadelphia or maybe Baltimore. Harry didn't exactly cut a dashing figure. Howard guessed he must have been in his sixties. The buttons of his baggy suit coat were always open to display red suspenders. He was under five-ten, a potbelly, chubby fingers, spindly legs. His hair was parted in the middle and plastered down on the sides of his head. Howard had never seen him without an Uncle Willie clinched in his teeth.

"If you're looking for stuff on politics," Howard said, "I got this book that came in yesterday. Guy who sold it to me said it's a study of the New Deal written by someone in Roosevelt's Brain Trust."

"Brain Drain, you mean. Roosevelt! That tin-horned messiah. That son of a bitch was responsible for our national debt, for every piece of highfalutin garbage in the law books, for every mountebank on the public payroll. . . ."

He took out a penknife, opened it, and began cleaning his fingernails.

"Wait a minute, Harry, that's FDR you're talking about! Folks on Fourth Avenue worshiped the ground he rolled his wheelchair on, including my old man."

"I refuse to say anything unkind about your dear, departed father, even though he did talk like a damned fool most of his life. But Herr Professor Doktor Roosevelt, that's another matter. He was like a snake-oil vendor in a broken-down carnival. Always wore that ingratiating grin on his face. And the same morals and the same sense of responsibility as a purveyor of leaches!"

"But FDR licked the Depression and ended the bread lines. I read it in the papers."

Harry snorted. "What's wrong with bread lines? Just think of the nobility of a good death from starvation. Besides, it seems to me that most of the boobs who died on the bread lines weren't worth having around anyway."

"And Roosevelt won us the war," Howard said. "Beat the shit out of the Japs and the Nazis, too."

"You've been reading the front pages of the tabloids too long, my friend. Dr. R was in the grave when the surrender came and was practically in the grave when he started the whole thing to begin with. And frankly, I could care less who won the war. I'd be just as content with that two-bit goose-stepping moron in the baggy pants as with some crippled old man and his homely wife. I've always said that what this country needs is an absolute monarchy. Dr. R should have been the first to take the throne. He would have been every bit as good a king as he was bad as a president."

Harry began to sneeze.

"Damned allergies," he said. "Here it is, blazing hot and I'm sneezing like I have pneumonia. Took my temperature three times this morning. I seem to be oxidizing. I think the equipment is wearing out. And I have to go to Philadelphia. If that won't take me home on a shutter, nothing will."

He dabbed at his brow with a yellowed handkerchief that he pulled from his back pocket, and went off to rummage through the bookshelves. Howard went back to his *Daily News*. Tojo had undergone his first two hours of cross-examination by allied prosecutors in his war crimes trial, insisting he acted out of loyalty to the emperor. Mayor O'Dwyer was trying to keep his parks commissioner, Robert Moses, in line. Truman had announced an anti-inflation effort by putting a team of cabinet members on it, headed by the chairman of the Council of Economic Advisers, who were supposed to report back to the Eighty-first Congress.

About time! Howard thought as he threw the tabloid in the general direction of a wastebasket. Inflation was getting out of control. Hamburger was thirty-eight cents a pound, turkey sixty-five cents, sirloin seventy-nine cents. Food was too damned expensive and hand-to-mouth guys like Howard and Jacob Bluestein were starting to hurt.

Then he remembered Lenny Gould's manuscript and he could almost hear the clink of silver dollars being shifted from palm to palm. But like Pop, Howard was not a guy to be rushed. He had given Lenny orders to cool the old lady. Keep her on ice until he thought things over. Raising four grand was no easy job. Besides, he was going to have to take a gander at that thing before making an investment. And in the back of his mind was the idea that maybe Lenny had stolen it.

That's exactly the point Howard had raised with Ann Elkin in her flat after a strenuous workout in her lumpy bed, pecked at by her goddamned canary that kept making kamikaze dives at his naked ass.

"Wake up, Howard," she said, shaking him. "You've got to go. I must get back to work."

He had taken her on a night on the town. They had gone to the Roxy, where Dan Dailey was starring in *When My Baby Smiles at Me* and Mickey Rooney was on the stage in person. Then they had stopped at the Red Coach Grill for some beers and the $2.50 lamb chops.

"Go home, Howard."

Home was Washington Heights. One hundred eighty-first Street near the G.W. Bridge. They were using the latest streamlined subway cars on the IND. Better lighting, fans to keep the straphangers cool. But at three o'clock in the morning, he'd rather stay in Hell's Kitchen with Ann Elkin than make excursions on the A train. He'd prefer to put up with the lumps in her bed three flights up in a floor-through with a bathtub in the kitchen. When she wasn't taking a bath, she kept the tub covered with an enamel top. He reached for a Chesterfield, which he smoked partly because he liked Betty Grable's gams in her cigarette ads in *Collier's* and *The Saturday Evening Post*.

"Howard, I've had a hell of a great Friday night. I mean, how often do you get to go to eat greasy lamb chops and see Mickey

Rooney, too? But some of us are artists and my art beckons. I've got to return to the Smith-Corona and the de' Medicis. Time's running out and Chirpy and I aren't getting any younger. I want to be on the set when Cecil B. De Mille calls the camera angles."

Howard exhaled.

"But we haven't talked about Lenny and that—"

"If Lenny hasn't stolen that thing, then it's a phony and you'll lose everything you have. It wouldn't surprise me if Lenny is mixed up with this man Larch."

"Who's Larch?

"You remember the theft at the Bottom Collection? The big man with the huge hands? It was Larch. Richard James Larch. Just as the police thought. Six months ago, he was arrested at Wittenberg College in Ohio for stealing books from its library. He jumped bail. He was almost caught again several weeks later at Haverford College in Pennsylvania. He was spotted by an alert librarian who recognized him from a description in a library professional magazine. He slugged the old man, pushed his way out, and took off in an Oldsmobile, like Mauri Rose. But I heard that he dropped a wallet that had a receipt from a hotel inside it. When the police got there, Larch was gone but he had left behind hundreds of index cards listing books and manuscripts that had been stolen from all over the country. Detailed bibliographic descriptions and codes that apparently indicate where the books are hidden. It was Larch's inventory! Or at least part of it. And there were several manuscripts mentioned on those cards, not unlike the one Lenny is trying to pawn off on you. It's scary knowing that Larch is out there somewhere carrying a gun. And that Lenny might be mixed up with him."

"You don't know that at all. It's just a guess. Lenny insists he's clean. On his mother's—"

"But isn't it a strange coincidence that Larch shows up in town at the same time Lenny comes along with this so-called priceless manuscript? Howard, you go along with Lenny and you're going to get taken one way or the other."

"You just said that you and the canary aren't getting any younger.

Well, I'm getting gray hairs, too. I need a break. One of these days, and I mean soon, I want to shut the door on Fourth Avenue and retire to the Cross Winds Hotel. If I don't try to do something now . . ."

Ann Elkin just shook her head.

"And if it *is* legit," he said, "and I don't move pretty quick, then Lenny's going to give up on me and take it to his cockeyed friend Ronald Newberry."

"Then Newberry would be the fool. Better him than you. At least he can afford to lose four thousand dollars. You can't. Now, Howard it's—"

"I know. I know. But how about a bath first? Let's go to the kitchen and take the top off the tub."

She threw him out. No bath. A fast kiss on the lips to seal the good-bye. He could hear her typewriter almost as soon as his oxfords touched the first step of the stairs and he creaked his way down to Fifty-first Street. So much for his Friday night and his dilemma still unsolved. What would Pop have done?

Harry plunked a battered copy of *Huckleberry Finn* on the counter.

"Something to read on the train," he said. "In fact, I read it once a year without fail. It's one of the five great masterpieces of the world. Fully the equal of *Don Quixote* or *Robinson Crusoe* and vastly the superior of *Tristram Shandy* or *Nicholas Nickleby* or *Tom Jones*. I solemnly believe it will be read by all humans over and over, not as a duty, but for the honest love of it long after every other book written in America has disappeared, except those that serve as classroom fossils. Old Mark Twain! There's an American for you, a Yankee right from the roots. And yet here in New York, where literary criminals presume to command our culture, Twain is depicted as a smut peddler. How much?"

"For you, a quarter."

He pulled a coin from his pocket and handed it to Howard. Then he extracted a soda mint from the breast pocket of his jacket and swallowed it. He gulped in relief as the mint began to soothe his obviously troubled stomach.

"Harry, I'm not sure about Twain, but it's bad business to sell smut. And illegal, too."

"What do you mean by smut, sir?"

"The stuff you're not allowed to sell. You can get into trouble, arrested. I mean we gotta vice squad here."

"In the city of Boston, which I might add is the asshole of the nation, I was once placed under arrest by official buffoons who accused me of violating Chapter two hundred seventy-two, section twenty-eight, of the Public General Laws, possessing and selling obscene literature. To wit, the sale of a magazine that included an article scornful of the Methodist Church. The morons who composed the Watch and Ward Society hauled me into court, where the judge ordered that the testimony be conducted in whispers so the audience couldn't hear it. It was about obscenity, after all! The only thing obscene was the show the good citizenry of Boston rehearsed."

"So what happened?"

"What happened was that the judge, presumably more enlightened than the average Bostonian, said that he had read the article in question and couldn't imagine anyone reading it and finding himself attracted toward vice. *Next case!*"

Harry pulled out another cigar from his breast pocket and stoked it. He seemed a little more mellow than when he first came into the store. Maybe now was the time.

"Say, Harry, you knew my old man a long time," Howard said. "I been thinking. I need some advice. Maybe you can help me."

"That remains to be seen."

"I got this buddy, see. He's like one of the family. Goes to CCNY. Now, he knows how to latch on to this manuscript. A hell of an old one. Not a book but a manuscript. Something some guy actually wrote by hand."

"I am aware of what manuscripts are."

"If I buy it, it's going to cost me a pretty penny. Everything I own and more. But if I can sell it to one of those big libraries or a museum or a university, I'd make a fortune. Whad'ya think?"

"You could also invest your life savings in the stock market and hope it's not 1929. However, book dealers are in the business of trading in bibliographic material, so why should you be any different? What is this document all about?"

"Well, my friend Lenny says it was written in 1790 by this English guy, see. William Trevor Coxe, who was in Paris at the start of the French Revolution."

"Interesting."

"Now my guy tells me Coxe had good connections with George the Third and Louis the Sixteenth, even though France and England weren't getting along so well right then. It's one hell of an important political and historical document. At least, that's what Lenny says, and he goes to CCNY and studies history. This big-shot dealer uptown is interested in it. Says the British Museum needs it to complete a collection of stuff about the French Revolution."

"And you have the capital to buy it?"

"Not exactly. I'd have to do a lot of scraping and selling and borrowing."

"Have you seen this purported manuscript?"

"Not yet. But Lenny knows where he can get his hands on it."

"And you are convinced it is genuine?"

"Lenny says so. And Ronald Newberry—he's the dealer—says it's been around for many years but no one knows just where. I've looked at some of these manuscripts and I know what they go for. Whad'ya think? Is it the real thing?"

"My dear sir, I wouldn't have the slightest idea about whether that document is genuine. And I am not an expert on the French Revolution, so I certainly cannot comment on its historical significance. I have never heard of a William Trevor Coxe, although I once knew a Franklin Baxter Coxe when I was going to Poly in Baltimore. However, it does sound enticing. How much do you believe you can make if you sell it?"

"Lenny thinks I can get eight or ten g's."

"Perhaps you should seek out some scholar who knows that period of French history."

"Well, Lenny knows all about it."

"Pray, then why go further? And why ask my advice?"

"I thought maybe you could have a look-see. If I had Lenny bring it down . . ."

"Certainly not."

"I don't want to be taken."

"I have a four-o'clock train to catch, so I'm not lingering to investigate the authenticity of some dubious manuscript."

Harry puffed his Uncle Willie and the smoke billowed around his head. Perhaps he read the disappointment on Howard's face through the smoke.

"I understand there are scientific ways to establish the age of a document," he told the book dealer. "Analyzing the paper and the ink to ensure they coincide with the period represented by the manuscript. Although all that is out of my realm. I am a pundit, not a laboratory technician."

"Are you saying it could be a fake?"

"Or a forgery."

"What's the difference?"

"I understand that a true forgery is a bogus object that had never existed before, something created by the forger from scratch. For example, a printed book that turns up by a famous author, say an 'undiscovered' work of Mark Twain. And yet it was a forger who put word to page, not old Mark. A fake, on the other hand, is an exact copy of an existing work, passed on with the intent of deceiving a buyer into believing that it is an original. The art world is filled with prints and paintings that are alleged to be by famous artists but which are just fakes. Even the experts have been fooled. As I recall, the man said to be the most infamous literary forger of all time was a London businessman named Thomas James Wise who produced totally forged works by Browning, Tennyson, Dickens, Kipling, and others. Wise was exposed by a couple of shrewed literary sleuths in 1934. However, from what you tell me, your manuscript appears to be authentic. I suppose the key question is what its true value is and whether you should invest. Indeed, just because it is old doesn't necessarily make it valuable."

"I just thought that if *anybody* would know . . ."

Harry pulled out a note pad and peeled off a blank piece of paper.

"In deference to your father, I'm putting down my address," he said in his gravelly voice. "If you find out more about the manuscript and contact me, I'll do what I can to determine its authenticity and perhaps help you locate a buyer." He belched some smoke. "By the way, is there any reason secondhand booksellers never clean their fingernails? Now I'm off to the nearest watering hole for a Michelob and then to Pennsylvania Station."

Harry sauntered out of the door and onto Fourth Avenue with his *Huckleberry Finn* under his arm. Howard looked at his fingernails. He did keep them clean, he thought. Well, tried to. It's just that with all those dusty books . . . He felt a thump on his leg. It was Brummell demanding something to eat. The cat spat. It was his usual way of being friendly. Howard opened a can of tuna fish and Brummell buried his face in it. Then he remembered the *Cabbages and Kings* Harry had sold him. It wasn't worth much, so he took it to the sidewalk to put it next to the other one on the card table. Damned if the first O. Henry wasn't gone! He rummaged around through the books on the table and sure enough it wasn't there. Jesus, that was the first time he'd ever had a book stolen from outside. Then he looked at the copy he was holding. It seemed remarkably familiar.

Now, he knew that old Harry wouldn't have sold Howard his own book. Harry wasn't *that* kind of guy.

6

Jacob Bluestein put the Dixie cup full of booze to his cracked lips and drained it in a single swallow.

"Howard, the time has come," he said, breathing out the alcohol fumes. "I been saving up for it and this time it's for sure. I'm gonna get myself one of those goddamned television sets so that I can watch it in my rocking chair in my room."

"Too expensive, Jacob."

"So is this booze but I drink it anyway!" At five sixty-five a fifth, Dewer's wasn't cheap, not even by 1948 standards. Neither Bluestein nor Howard's old man would ever skimp in the booze department.

"I've been putting the dough aside," Jacob said. "I'm gonna have May's department store deliver me a Crosley. It's four hundred forty-five plus installation."

"Shit, Jacob. That's half of your retirement money. Do like I do. Go to the Blarney Rock. Sit on a stool, nurse yourself a beer and nibble on some smokies, and watch TV for as long as you want."

"I'm too old to sit around saloons just to watch TV."

"You should wait for color."

"Hell, by the time they invent color, I'll be pushing up daffodils along with your old man. I'm getting me a Crosley so's I can see Arthur Godfrey's 'Talent Scouts' and 'Cap'ns Billy's Mississippi Music Hall' and watch Douglas Edwards read me the news."

"TV's a fad, Jacob. All the experts say so. Even if it catches on, it's just going to be a toy for the rich. Who's gonna have the patience and sit there and *watch* some guy read the news on TV when you can *hear* it on radio and do other things at the same time! And when you listen to 'The Lux Radio Theater' it comes out perfect. On TV, the props and scenery are always falling down and the actors are forgetting their lines. On radio, you know what you're gonna to get. Besides, even on the big screen at the Blarney Rock, there's terrible reception, all those ghosts and shadows and lines and snow. Radio comes in perfect."

"Dammit, don't try to talk me out of it. I sit here on Fourth Avenue every goddamned day and weekends, too, closed in by dirty, dusty books. I want to go home to my room, open myself a beer, fry myself a couple of sausages, turn on the Crosley, and crawl inside. I want to leave that crutch outside along with the smell of mustard gas that's still in my system and all the goddamned pain and everything else. Yessir, I'm going to May's first thing tomorrow and get me a Crosley. I got the money and nobody's going to talk me out of it."

Howard helped Jacob Bluestein put the SORRY WE'RE CLOSED sign on his door and watched as he hobbled furiously down Fourth Avenue to St. Mark's Place. Just off Avenue A, Jacob had a basement room next to the super's. Howard always wondered what Bluestein did there in that room all alone, just him and that crutch. Soon he would have a new roommate named Crosley.

The summer was almost over and Harry hadn't been back to the store. Maybe it was too hot. Even as early as June, record crowds were turning out at the beaches. The *Daily News* said there were 900,000 at Coney Island, 200,000 at the Rockaways, and 75,000 at Jones Beach. Howard knew old Harry wasn't one of them. He wasn't the kind of bird who took up sunbathing. Harry must have been monitoring the conventions, though, from wherever he was. They were on television for the first time and Howard watched WJZ-TV, Channel 7, at the Blarney Rock every night after he closed up the shop. The Republicans had their bash in Philadelphia and chose Dewey. The Democrats went there, too, and named Truman. And then there was poor crazy Henry Wallace for the Progressives.

"Everyone named Henry ought to be put to death," Harry told Pop. "And if someone will do it for Henry Wallace, then I promise to commit suicide."

Howard's old man fumed and snorted. He was a big admirer of Henry Wallace.

"You are a partisan, sir; I am completely neutral," Harry said. "I'm against all politicians."

"That's crap, Harry!" Pop sputtered between his dentures. "No matter what you think about the politicians we gotta have them. They're our elected representatives. Bad or good, they carry our will to city hall, the statehouse, and the White House. And besides, for every bad politician, there's a good one."

Harry lighted up a cigar and shook his head. "A false assumption, my book-mongering cohort. If history has taught us anything, it is that a good politician is as rare as an honest bank robber. The politician's very existence is a subversion of the public good. He does not serve the commonweal; he steals from it. If there is any honest and altruistic politician in America, I would like to meet him."

"Then what the hell would you do, Harry?" Pop screamed. "Execute anyone who ran for office?"

"Hmmm. The thought is tempting. But, no, not in every case. I agree that the politician, even at his ideal best, is a necessary evil. At his worst, he is an intolerable nuisance. Therefore, it is in our interest to hold the politician's powers to an irreducible minimum. To slash his compensation to zero. In my opinion, were we to regard him in the cold light of reason, then three-quarters of his obnoxiousness would disappear. He would still be a pest but no longer a mountebank. But before you conclude that I am too hard on the politician for his incurably antisocial behavior, there are other callings that are even worse. The career soldier, for example. He's nothing more than a professional murderer and kidnapper. Or the clergyman whose specialty is no different from that of an astrologer, a witch doctor, or a chiropractor. No, compared to them, the politician is a mere swindler and a sneak thief."

Pop snorted in disgust. "Harry, you've been to a political convention or two—"

"My dear, sir, I have been to every major political convention since 1904. I consider myself a specialist in political, homiletical, and patri-inspirational orgies."

"Then you've seen democracy in action!"

"I have seen a throng of reigning clowns, that's what I've seen. A mob of animals in a cage, pacing from one corner to the next. A spectacle about as amusing as a hanging. A carnival of buncombe!"

"You ever make a mistake, Harry? Once in your life did you ever make a mistake?"

"My dear merchant, I am human, you know. I did err once or twice. Let me see ... Oh yes! I recall that in 1924 I went to the Democratic Convention in my guise as a journalist. The show was a farce. Stalemated for more than a hundred ballots. Nevertheless, deadline approached, so I typed my lead. 'No one is sure about this convention except for one thing. John W. Davis will never be nominated.' I phoned it in. A few minutes later, I found that the convention had swung to Davis. Impossible! And I had already sent off the story. Just one thing ran through my mind. Would those idiots in Baltimore know enough to strike out the negative?"

Howard's old man laughed. "Yeah, you are human, Harry, but you're also a hater."

Harry shook his head.

"That's right, Harry, you are a man who hates everything. Everything!"

"I don't care how you describe me, sir, as long as you don't characterize me as some old dodo, late of the dissecting room. However, I do deny that I hate everything. I am in support of common sense, common honesty, and common decency. And that alone makes me ineligible to hold public office anywhere in the forty-eight states and the District of Columbia."

Harry.

"Bah-bah-bah," Howard could hear him say.

All the while during that political summer, he couldn't get that damned piece of paper out of his mind, the one Lenny Gould was so eager to get him to buy. Lenny with all his talk did wear him down; there was no question about that, but in the long run it was Howard's own decision. Bucks were bucks, especially when they were big ones.

"Okay, Lenny," Howard wearily told him one morning after ringing the cash register just four times for a grand total of two dollars and seventy-five cents. "I've decided I'll take a gander at that thing. Let's head up to Riverside Drive and have it out with this old lady friend of yours."

Lenny's eyes widened behind his horned-rims. "No, no, we can't do that. You'll have to come up to *my* place to look at it."

"I want to see this old gal for myself."

"Impossible. She demands anonymity."

"What's that?"

"She's keeping her identity a secret."

"From who?"

"From everyone. She's practically a recluse. Look, I'll go to her apartment and pick up the manuscript and let you check it out for yourself. But it'll have to be at my place only. It's too valuable to carry around all over New York County."

Howard scratched his head.

"All right, Lenny. I'm taking a chance on you. You get a hold of that thing and I'll be up to your place tonight. I wanna see it for myself."

Lenny shot out the door, picking at a pimple.

7

He poured some dried food into Brummell's bowl and stuck the CLOSED sign on the front door. At Fourteenth Street, he grabbed the Canarsie BMT and took it to its last stop in Manhattan, Eighth Avenue, where he changed and hopped a local up to Fiftieth Street and walked the rest of the way to Ann Elkin's.

"Great news, Howard!" she said as she greeted him at the top of the stairs. "We've got to celebrate!"

He saw a blur of yellow shoot over her head and then flutter down to her shoulder.

"Someday that damned bird's going to fly the coop," he said.

"Come in, Howard. Forget Chirpy. He doesn't go anywhere without me."

Ann Elkin shut the door and threw her arms around him.

"I'm going to be rich, Howard. *We're* going to be rich!"

"You sold it! The novel!"

"Almost. Edgar likes what he's seen so far and wants more."

"Edgar?"

"Edgar Ardery. He's my editor at Macmillan."

"And he wants more? You've already written seven hundred pages."

"Howard, I'm close. So close. He wants some changes. Instead of Florentine Italy, he's talking about Greece in the time of Alexander, about 330 B.C."

"But . . ."

"I know it's a major change in time and place. But he loves my heroine. He doesn't want to touch her. She runs a brothel in Athens but becomes the brains and the power behind the Republic. Edgar adores her."

"Decent of him. Look, I'm not up on all this writing and stuff but it seems to me that Macmillan's asking too much. They're changing everything."

"Let's celebrate, you big palooka. I've put some champagne in the Frigidaire."

"Your Edgar hasn't said he'd buy it!"

"He as much as did. It's just rewriting. I'm going to start tonight. What do you think about Helen?"

"Helen?"

"My heroine's name. Edgar wants me to use Helen."

"But . . ."

"I know. It *was* Andrea. But Helen is beautiful, don't you think?"

She popped the champagne and the cork shot into the air, just missing the canary.

"Ann . . ."

"A toast, Howard!"

"Seven hundred pages, Ann. Now you're starting from scratch. Another era. Different country. New names. Everything. Why don't you look for another publisher?"

"You know what Macmillan did for *Gone With the Wind*. Edgar will do the same for me. Only better."

"Is he offering you anything? An advance?"

"That's only for established writers, Howard. And Helen will be what will establish me. Let's toast Helen and us and Edgar and Macmillan."

"There's another manuscript we ought to toast," he said.

"Which one?"

"Lenny's."

"Christ, Howard, don't be a fool about that. I told you to forget Lenny's manuscript." Her eyes narrowed. She lighted a Pall Mall.

They finished the bottle. It tasted flat. Suddenly everything seemed to turn into a wake instead of a celebration. The canary flew down to Ann's glass and perched on the rim to dip its beak in the wine. He had never heard Chirpy sing. Maybe Chirpy was waiting for Ann to sell the big one before the bird burst into song.

Howard was a little high from Ann Elkin's champagne when he got up to Lenny's place on East 106th Street. Lenny had lived in the five-story walk-up with his ma until she died, and then he moved into a smaller flat on the third floor. There were mostly old Jews and Irish and Germans in the tenement but Howard had a feeling that was going to change. Bodegas were springing up in the neighborhood and that meant Puerto Ricans were moving in.

Lenny's room smelled like dirty socks, which made sense because that's the way Lenny smelled sometimes. There were piles of clothes strewn around the room just where Lenny had dropped them. And stacks of books, most of them borrowed from 80½.

"Dammit, Lenny. I told you to take those books back to the store. How can I make a living if you keep bringing them up here to read?"

"For college, Howard, college. You know I can barely afford textbooks. I'll take them back. Now, sit down. I've got what you've come to see."

He went to a closet and removed from under a pile of suits and coats a cardboard box that he carried as delicately as a Fabergé Easter egg. With care he opened the lid of the box and removed a stack of oversized pages, maybe fifteen by twelve inches of yellowed parchment. On the first page in finely scripted handwriting were the words, *An Englishman's Account of the Revolution of 1789 and the Taking of the Bastille.* Under it was the name of William Trevor Coxe. And then the words, "written in his hand 1790."

"Easy," Lenny warned. He gnawed at his thumbnail. "This document is in remarkably good condition but if anything happens to it—"

"I'm careful, I'm careful."

"You don't know what I went through to get this manuscript. Thank God the old lady trusts me. But I've got to get it back to her tonight. I mean like within the hour."

It was old all right. Had all this crazy spelling. All the s's looked like f's.

"How do you read this damned thing?"

"It's easy when you get used to it. Let me read you some of it."

I had been to Paris [Lenny read] twice the previous fall and was quite familiar with its fortifications, not to mention its many stores, cafes, and places of revelry. The people of Paris were in a mood for insurrection and there had twice been near-engagements with troops under the marshal de Broglio following the plan of the duke of Coigny who had distributed his forces around the capitol. He had crowded his infantry into three or four little camps on natural ponds near the city; his cavalry occupied two well-planned parks in Grenelle and St. Denys, and his large artillery arrived in the later place. He had only thrown a garrison of fifty Swiss guards into the Bastille. I told de Coigny that if they persevered in maintaining so absurd and unmilitary a position, they would most assuredly be beaten; that the defection of the French guards ought to serve as an example of the folly of placing the troops so near the women of the town, the seduction of good cheer, and the blandishments of the Palais-royal. Had by proper means the Bastille been fortified Paris would have been blockaded and the King saved. I do not mean to moralize but had I been in command my first movement would have been to ensure the person of Louis XVI.

The American War did not form great generals among the French and while I do not wish to belittle the young men employed in it, it should be said that they had the opportunity of examining a new people who were governed by an influential constitution. I state this boldly despite my unfamiliarity with America. The heads of the French troops had been made giddy by those backwoodsmen. They returned to France with ill-digested ideas and wishing to adapt them to the national genius, they set on fire, and lighted up a volcano which covered France with ruins and rubbish.

"What do you think?" Lenny asked. "Fascinating stuff, huh? If they had listened to Coxe, the Bastille might not have fallen and Louis the Sixteenth and Marie Antoinette might not have lost their heads under the guillotine along with about seventeen thousand other loyalists."

Howard was impressed all right. But he still wasn't sure what all of that stuff meant.

"But is it really history?" he asked.

"Howard, *of course* it's history. Listen, Coxe is saying that he had gone to Paris twice as a military observer and checked out not only all of its fortifications but all of its places of sin, too. Coxe could smell revolt in the air. There had already been a number of near clashes with the forces of the king, whose officers had only crudely fortified the Bastille and left Louis virtually unprotected. At the same time, Coxe is saying that the French rebels were about to take a cue from the American Revolution, that those who fought against the British on the side of the Americans came back to France predisposed to overthrow the throne. It's a marvelous firsthand account of that era, a remarkable document."

Howard was bitten. Maybe, sitting under that bare forty-watt light bulb dangling from Lenny's ceiling and hearing Lenny read, a spell was cast. Maybe it was Ann Elkin's champagne. Maybe the thought of how he could turn that manuscript into ten grand. Maybe because touching it felt good, the paper smooth, not brittle, just a little turned at the edges.

"I can't believe it's so old," he said.

"Oh, it's old all right. See, there's a lot of acid content in paper made these days. Paper is cheap. That's why New York's got a dozen daily newspapers. See all these books lying around? I know,

I know. I'm going to take them back to the shop! Give me time. Well, those books taught me a lot. And not only about the French Revolution but about how books are made. For example, I know that until 1860 virtually all paper was made out of rags. Cloth. Then the English began having a rag shortage. So they started using straw to make their paper. Then they used esparto grass. By—"

"Wait a minute, wait a minute," Howard interrupted. "What the hell is this esparto grass?"

"Oh, specially grown grass in southern Europe or northern Africa expressly for making paper—or cord."

"Never heard of no esparto grass."

"They grew it, Howard. Anyway, by the time the Industrial Revolution was in its heyday, all sorts of new papermaking techniques developed using chemical pulp processes. Some day they might even be able to make paper from synthetic chemicals. All that means is that the paper you've been touching with your hand, that marvelous document by Mr. Coxe, will last a hell of a lot longer than any book printed on today's paper. It's still got to be taken care of. Say I run out and spend a nickel on a Coke and bring it back and spill it on Mr. Coxe's masterpiece. It won't survive that. It looks old, Howard, and it is old. But it's not going to crumble in your hand like last year's newspaper. It'll last longer than you will—and certainly more than long enough for you to find the right buyer. A rich one."

"It's a deal, Lenny."

"Cash first, Howard."

"What?"

"*Cash*. That's what the old lady wants and that's what I promised. Now."

"Jesus, Lenny, I can't get all that cash together right away."

"Next week then."

"I'm not sure about next week, a few weeks, maybe."

"Howard, you're my best friend in all the world. You're like a brother to me. There's nothing I wouldn't do for you. But there's another party involved in this deal and she wants her money. You get that four grand together in cash and we're home free. This thing has been stretching out too long. I could have gone to Ronald Newberry anytime over the summer. But I didn't. I was waiting for you!"

He left Lenny and the forty-watt bulb and the smell of his socks behind and almost eagerly hopped the subway. For the first time in his ordinary life, he was about to invest in something that would change things.

Forever.

8

He was busy as hell over the next few weeks, almost too busy to sell books. He picked up his Nash in Hoboken and sold it for $145 to a used-car dealer on Hudson Boulevard, not far from the Holland Tunnel. Then he went over to the good old First National on Thirty-fourth Street and explained to the loan officer how he was expanding the store's inventory and needed two grand right away.

The banker peered over his glasses at him and decided that since Howard was an established merchant, the bank could go for maybe fifteen hundred and that the money could be claimed in due course. Mister Banker didn't know that Howard planned to clean out his savings account when he picked up that fifteen hundred. No need to jeopardize his relationship with his friend the loan officer. He might want more someday.

He pawned his ma's jewelry at an Eighth Avenue hockshop. Sold all his furniture, except for his bed, to a secondhand dealer on Canal Street. Went to Amsterdam Avenue to hit old Butterman for a loan. Butterman had made a fortune on funerals and since he liked Howard's pop, he came up with a couple of hundred for old time's sake. As time passed, it became clear that he was going to make it. Four grand and a little more.

He had read in the *Daily News* that the average nonfarm income in 1947, the year before, was about $2,500 a year. So despite the prices cockeyed Ronald Newberry demanded for his goods, four thousand bucks was a pile of dough by anyone's standards.

He was in and out of 80½ for days and didn't sell a damned thing. He was too preoccupied with raising money.

"Say, Lenny, I got a question!" Howard grabbed the kid one day as Lenny was dashing through the store. "I know how you met Newberry but just how did you latch on to this old lady anyway?"

Lenny unwrapped a Tootsie Roll and stuffed it in his mouth, letting the paper wrapper float to the floor.

"Howard," he said, his mouth full, "you've been like a brother to me but there are things that I simply cannot go into. But the fact of the matter is, I learned of the manuscript's existence while I was working up at Caesar's."

"You sure you didn't rob this old lady?"

"Howard we've been through all this . . ."

"Like take advantage of her somehow?"

"On my . . ."

"You take her to bed or something?"

"For Christ's sake, Howard, she's close to ninety!"

"Yeah, well a kid who's as ugly as you are can't be too choosy."

At last, the grinning loan officer at First National presented Howard with a fifteen-hundred-dollar check. The old biddy in the teller's cage was a little startled when he told her to give him the money in cash, hundred-dollar bills. After she did, he wiped out his savings account and carried his new fortune back to 80½ in a brown paper bag.

Behind the locked door, he spread all the money he had raised on the counter. He had never seen so much at one time and in one place. Most in one-hundred-dollar bills. He rolled the bills neatly and put a rubber band around them. It was a nice, fat wad that he stuffed into an old argyle sock. He reached under the counter and grabbed the Dewar's from its familiar spot and blew the dust off it. He figured that if he was going to turn all that dough over to Lenny, he might as well take a bottle with him so they could celebrate.

He hopped a number 6 train to 103rd Street, where he got off and walked through the brisk end-of-fall air to Lenny's rooming house on 106th. Outside Lenny's place, a couple of old guys sitting on upturned soap boxes were moving checkers on a board balanced on the lid of a garbage pail.

"King me!" one of them said and winked as Howard walked up the stoop to ring Lenny's bell.

"I knew you'd come," Lenny said as he opened his door. "It's here."

"It better be. I been bustin' my ass to raise all that cash. Why is it I feel like I'm doing something wrong?"

"It's the right thing to do. You won't regret it."

He handed Lenny the argyle sock. Funny. Four g's didn't look all that big rolled up in a sock. Lenny shook the sock and the roll tumbled out onto his bed. He took the rubber band off and counted the bills. Twice. He shook his head in satisfaction. Lenny rolled the bills again and replaced them in the sock that he stashed under his mattress. Then he went to the closet to get the manuscript from its hiding place while Howard poured himself a Scotch in one of Lenny's cloudy-looking glasses.

"Have one," Howard said.

"You know me, Howard. Never touch it."

Howard took the Coxe document out of its box and gloated over it, carefully turning the pages and holding them up to the light, such as it was. Lenny wasn't big on illumination, which is maybe why his eyes were so bad.

"We still got work to do, Lenny."

"I know."

"I expect to make a profit on this deal."

"I know you do, Howard."

He left Lenny's carrying the box with the manuscript under his arm. He was almost going to spring for a cab, thanks to the long green he had leftover, but then he saw P. J. Murphy's on the corner and decided to stop in for a quickie. Not that he wasn't already feeling just fine, courtesy of the Scotch warming his belly. He scooted up to the mahogany bar and had a couple of beers while on the Dumont he watched Rex Barney of the Dodgers pitch a no-hitter against the Giants. He wasn't much of a baseball fan but you don't see no-hitters that often. He didn't forget the manuscript. It was right beside him on a bar stool, safe in its box, all held together with rubber bands. He was feeling no pain when he staggered out to Lexington Avenue to grab a cab. He really wanted to head downtown and Ann Elkin's place but was a little too loaded for that. She sure as hell would toss him out. Nope. Had to be uptown for him. Back to good old Washington Heights, even if the only thing waiting there for him was a bed, an empty one. Then he remembered! The Dewar's. Shit! He had left it on Lenny's desk. Hell, he wasn't leaving a half-empty $5.65 fifth of Dewar's in the room of somebody who didn't drink. So he ran back to 106th Street. The front door was ajar, so he pushed it open and went inside instead of ringing Lenny's bell. He took the steps two at a time but slowed down when he got to the third-floor landing because he definitely had the feeling that something was wrong. Then he knew something was wrong. Lenny's door was partway open. Not open much. Just a crack, really, enough to let a little shaft of light into the hall.

"Lenny?" he asked. His voice was practically a whisper. He leaned the box with the Coxe manuscript on the floor against the wall of the dark hallway. Then he pushed the door open a little wider with his finger.

"Lenny?"

He peeked inside. Lenny's room was always such a rotten mess, he didn't notice at first. Then he realized a chair was on its side. A table was facedown on the floor, its legs sticking up. All the drawers of Lenny's desk were pulled out and there were papers everywhere. Books were strewn on the floor by the hundred. The closet door was open and everything inside had been thrown outside.

Jesus, he said to himself. Someone really tore up the place. He walked across the room as well as he could, stepping over the clutter of lamps and books and records and chairs. Then he saw Lenny in the bathroom. At first he thought Lenny was grinning at him as if to welcome him back. But Lenny wasn't grinning at all. His teeth were bared in a grimace that probably reflected the brief pain he once felt. His eyes looked at Howard without their glasses but they didn't see. There was a cord around Lenny's neck and it stretched up to the bar holding the shower curtain. Lenny's glasses were beside him, smashed on the floor. Lenny. Poor homely Lenny. Poor bright Lenny. Floating. Floating now from a cord. Howard stepped back, catching his foot on some fallen object on the floor, and almost fell on his ass. He sobered up in a hurry.

"*Where is it?*"

It was a deep voice, bellowing. And from behind the front door charged a huge shape. Howard felt a blow on his shoulder and spun into Lenny's desk. He saw his bottle of Dewar's topple and then fall from the desk with a crash. He could smell the unleashed whiskey fumes.

"Where is it? Dammit!"

The man was a giant. He grabbed Howard by the throat, lifted him from the floor, and then pitched him backward. Howard cracked into a chest whose drawers were jutting into the room and slid like a doomed prizefighter, down on the ring at three. The giant stood over him. A ham hock slapped his face. One way, then the other.

"Give it to me! Now. Or you'll wind up just like that kid in there. Give it to me, dammit!"

Howard wasn't sure what he was talking about. And he was scared.

"What?" he asked. "I don't know what you want."

"Don't play games with me!" he roared. "You two were in it together."

"The money. You want the money . . ."

"Bastard!"

"A sock. It's in a sock!"

"Liar!"

Then he felt the man's hands around his throat and the pressure as the fingers dug into his flesh. From under Lenny's forty-watt bulb, Howard could see the attacker's face and his enormous eyes and the silver-gray hair that seemed to catch the light and magnify it. Then there were two faces and four eyes and the hair began to blur with the same kind of movements you see from a car window on a rainy night. Instinctively, Howard's hands tried to force the attacker's away from his throat but he had no strength. He was fading and he knew it.

He thought he could hear a faraway voice. A high-pitched voice like that of a woman. Abruptly the pressure around his throat ended and he began to cough, gasping for breath at the same time. He felt his body slide farther down to the floor.

"Mister, Mister."

The woman's voice.

"Mister."

Then closer.

"Are you all right?"

His eyes began to focus. He saw a face, a woman's face, elderly, felt her hand on his arm, shaking him gently.

"He's gone. He ran off when he heard me at the door. I'm Mrs. Jacobson, the landlady. I heard all the commotion. Mister, try to get yourself up. Look, I found this box outside the door. Is it yours?"

"Larch," he said, grabbing the box. "Larch!"

"I'll get you some water and you just clear your throat again," she said.

"No, *Larch*. The man who tried to kill me. It was Larch. He killed Lenny. *Murdered* Lenny!"

"Mur . . ."

"Did you see a sock? A rolled-up sock. It has . . ."

"Mister, no one can find nothing in this mess. Did you say mur . . ."

"The bathroom."

She got up from her knees and went to the bathroom door.

Her scream lasted for a long time. Lenny was a homely kid and death didn't help.

9

"I'm Detective Sergeant Mulvey. Maybe you oughta go to the hospital, pal."

The police had taken Howard to the front parlor of the landlady's apartment downstairs, while up in Lenny's room the forensics officers dusted for fingerprints, took photographs, put little objects into plastic bags, and drew lines on the floor.

"No, I'm just a little shaken up," he told the the lanky cop who was wearing a wrinkled double-breasted business suit and a wide-brim hat. The box with the precious Coxe manuscript was next to Howard on a cloth-covered table, but the cops didn't seem to notice it. Maybe they thought it belonged to Mrs. Jacobson. He had made up his mind he wasn't going to tell them about it. They might take it away from him, use it as evidence or something. His life's savings were invested in that thing. He was going to have to hide it.

Howard knew he was doing a lot of things wrong. There were lots of reasons. Greed, of course, but also fear. The shock that came when something unexpected happened, something bad. Until he was lying next to Pop, he knew he'd never forget seeing Lenny hanging from that line like something in the window of a butcher shop. The killer might be back. Howard might end up the same way as Lenny. But he had to protect his investment. It was all he had left.

"Now, Mrs. Jacobson here says you told her you recognized the man who attacked you and murdered your friend," Mulvey said.

Howard was also keeping mum about his real relationship with Lenny. That could make things even worse, not to mention the promise he had made to his old man.

"Yeah, well, I never actually saw the killer before."

"But you identified him as a man called Larch."

"I think it was Larch. At least he looked like the guy my girlfriend described, the man who pulled off that robbery at the New York Public Library last month."

"Richard James Larch," Mulvey said. "I had the name checked out. He's wanted for grand larceny, conspiracy, assault, and crossing state lines to avoid prosecution. But as far as we know, he's never committed a murder before."

"He got off a shot at the library."

"True. Probably just a matter of time before he hurt someone."

Mulvey took out a Lucky Strike from a crumpled pack, then offered Howard one. He took it. Mulvey lit Howard's and then his, waved the flame from the match, and dropped it on Mrs. Jacobson's carpet. He paced the room a bit.

"You mentioned your lady friend."

"She works at the library."

"And she saw this Larch during the robbery there?"

"No, but she was in the building at the time. The cops told her what he looked like. And there are wanted posters in the post office."

"I'm just not sure what sort of connection this man Larch may have had with the victim."

"Me neither."

"Mr. Gould was employed by you, correct?"

"He worked in my store part-time. He was going to CCNY."

"You sell books."

"Secondhand."

"And this fugitive Larch *stole* books."

"He wouldn't have stolen any of mine. I just have nickel-and-dime stuff."

Mulvey flipped an ash from his cigarette onto Mrs. Jacobson's floor, then rubbed his chin to scratch the long-day's stubble.

"Just what sort of relationship did you have with Mr. Gould?"

"Terrific. I knew him since he was a kid."

"Then it was more than an employer-employee relationship."

"My Pop knew him, too."

"You ever have arguments with Mr. Gould?"

"With Lenny? Hell, all the time. Who didn't? He was a god-damned pain in the ass sometimes. But not enough to kill. I mean, all I had to do was just tell him to get lost and he'd get lost."

"What was the purpose of your visiting him tonight?"

"Sergeant, we were almost like, like brothers. We never had to have a *reason* to see each other. Besides, Lenny had a lot of used books he had borrowed from the store. So I thought I'd stop by and pick them up and also share a bottle of Scotch I had brought along."

"So your visit was mostly social in nature."

"Well, more or less. Book dealers always combine business with pleasure, such as it is."

"And when you entered Mr. Gould's apartment, you were attacked by this man Larch. Or by someone who resembles him."

"Right."

"Did Larch say anything to you before he attacked you?"

"Ah . . . no. Not really."

"Why do you suppose he attacked you?"

"I don't know. Didn't want to be caught. Or recognized. Mrs. Jacobson came just in time or I might be dead right now, too."

Mulvey exhaled. "Mrs. Jacobson verifies that a huge man was on top of you when she came into the apartment. It would appear that she frightened him off."

"She saved my life."

"Little frail woman like that. You wouldn't have thought a big man like that would have been afraid of her. He could have finished her off as easily as he did Mr. Gould. Or yourself."

"He probably panicked."

Mulvey exhaled again. "Why do you suppose Larch was in Mr. Gould's apartment to begin with?"

"Robbery."

"Think so?"

"Although I can't think of anything valuable Lenny might have had."

"Mr. Gould's apartment was ransacked. But the place is such a mess, it's impossible right now to determine what might have been taken, if anything." Mulvey walked to the front window of Mrs. Jacobson's parlor, parted the white curtains, and looked out onto East 106th Street. It had started to rain. The water reflected like a prism the red flashing light of a prowl car. "So there's nothing you can think of that Lenny Gould had that Larch may have wanted?"

"Lenny never owned very much. Except books, of course, and most of those he borrowed from me. But Larch wouldn't kill Lenny for any of those."

"Tell me, Mr . . ."

"Call me Howard."

"Mr. Howard—"

"No, it's—"

". . . was Lenny a homosexual?"

"Lenny? Jesus, I don't think he was a queer. I never saw him with any girl. But he was too ugly for a boy to like, either."

"And you, pal?"

"Me what?"

"I think you know what I'm asking."

"Christ, I'm no fag. I gotta girlfriend. You don't think there's any fairy connection?"

"Anything is possible."

"And this guy Larch. A homosexual?"

"We're checking it." He dropped his cigarette on Mrs. Jacobson's carpet and flattened the butt with his heel. The heel was worndown.

"Just one more thing, Mr. Howard." Mulvey's voice was filled with sarcasm. "Don't leave town. You'll be hearing from us."

Christ, it was like being in a John Garfield movie.

One of Mulvey's squad cars drove Howard through the rain to West 181st Street. His head was pounding, his throat raw. He had hidden the box with the Coxe manuscript under the draped table in Mrs. Jacobson's living room, intending to go back after it in the next day or two. He was counting on the hope that Mrs. Jacobson didn't sweep too often. At least not under her table. He went upstairs to his empty room. The only thing he had left was his bed and his clothes. There wasn't even a table or a chair. He had sold everything else to raise the money for his dream. He dropped his shoes and hit the unmade sheets without undressing or taking off his hearing aid, and was asleep within seconds. Not a real sleep, but one in which he was semi-awake but still had bizarre dreams, nightmares really.

There was Lenny Gould's body spinning like a top, round and round, faster and faster. Then he saw his old man rising up out of the grave, pointing his finger, crying, "Howard, why did you get involved in this thing, Howard? Why, Howard?" Brummell was clawing at him. And there was old Harry, a cigar at the corner of his mouth, saying, "you are a poltroon, sir, a boob, a pathetic dullard." Then Ann Elkin, slapping his face. Forward then backward. Chirpy shitting white on his shoulder. And Jacob Bluestein, raising his crutch and bringing it down on his head. Again. And again.

In his half-sleep from faraway, he thought he heard a noise, like a series of clicks. A lock, maybe, or a doorknob turning. Suddenly he sat upright in his bed. That noise! Someone at his door. He got out of the bed and padded in his socks over to the wall switch and turned it on. He put his ear to the door but he didn't hear anything. He fumbled with his hearing aid, turning it up full blast. Then he did hear something. A heavy foot on the stairs outside and a few seconds later, the closing of the foyer door. Someone had tried to get into his apartment. Maybe. He wasn't sure. But he wasn't going to go outside and check. It might have been Larch, back to kill Howard the way he did Lenny. Come to get the William Trevor Coxe manuscript, the thing that got Lenny strung up in the first place. He bolted the door with the inside chain and leaned against it, breathing heavily. He sank to the floor and somehow fell asleep.

That week, Mulvey or one of his flunkies talked to Howard a few more times and he told them almost everything, but nothing he thought would jeopardize the manuscript. They also questioned Ann Elkin and Jacob Bluestein and Klein the Landlord and the folks at CCNY and just about everyone else Lenny knew, which weren't many. As Howard knew she would, Ann kept her mouth shut about the Coxe document and about his real relationship with Lenny.

He was scared.

When he walked to the subway, he kept looking over his shoulder, trying to spot Larch in the crowd. The giant had tried to kill Howard once. He might try again. Howard passed a taxicab near Union Square and from its open window, he could hear the cabbie listening to "Nature Boy" on his radio. It was 1948's number-one song. Melancholy. Like his thoughts about Lenny.

The cops wouldn't release Lenny's body from the morgue until after an autopsy, but Howard arranged for it to be taken to Butterman's funeral home on Amsterdam Avenue and Seventy-sixth Street. It was going to be a small service. Just a few of the booksellers from Fourth Avenue. He decided to have Lenny buried next to his ma in Woodlawn Cemetery in the Bronx. Somebody had to make the arrangements. He was the only family Lenny had, even if he couldn't admit it.

10

On Tuesday, he opened the store as usual. A guy came in and bought Dale Carnegie's *How to Win Friends and Influence People.* Then some lady picked out a *Ben Hur.* He got rid of a couple of copies of *National Geographic.* $3.85. Thank God it was slow because he had real business to do. So in the afternoon, he put the CLOSED sign on the door and hopped a number 4 train to Fulton Street downtown. Then he caught an A up to Washington Square, where he changed to a D to Columbus Circle. He switched to a local to 110th, where he went above ground to take a crosstown bus over to Third Avenue. He wasn't taking any chances. He didn't want to be followed by Mulvey or by Larch.

East 106th Street was its usual self. Some kids playing stickball.

The two old guys he had seen before were still there, coat collars raised against a chill wind, moving checkers around on a board setting on a garbage pail lid. Some old ladies in babushkas gabbing on the stoop. A few Puerto Ricans drinking cheap wine from paper bags in a urine-stained doorway. The odor of the wine and the odor of the urine were almost the same. There was no action at all outside the house where Lenny had lived. And died. No cop standing guard or anything. You'd never have known murder had been done there. He went up to the foyer and rang Mrs. Jacobson's bell. She recognized him right away through the door's curtained window.

"Mrs. Jacobson, I just came over to thank you for saving my life. You arrived just in time. I was almost a goner. Wouldn't be here right now if it wasn't for you."

"Ah, Mister, I didn't do nothing anybody else wouldn't have done. You didn't have to come all the way here to tell me that. Come in and have some tea."

He sat in the chair next to the draped table. The same chair he had been in when Mulvey had questioned him. Mrs. Jacobson poured a cup of weak brew. There was a menorah on a velvet-covered table against the wall.

"I did want to ask you," she said, "when the police officers allow us back in, are you going to clean out poor Mr. Gould's room? I mean there is an awful lot of books and things up there. And I'm going to have to rent it again. That is, if I can find anyone who wants to live in a place where there's been a dead person. Some people is superstitious, you know."

"Sure, Mrs. Jacobson. I'll go in and clear it out just as soon as the cops give the go-ahead. Most of those books belong downtown anyway."

He sipped the tea slowly, wondering whether he should reach under the table, grab the manuscript, and run out or be right up front about it. It didn't pay to make her suspicious.

"By the way, Mrs. Jacobson, I seem to remember having left something here. In your parlor. A box. I forgot about it in all the excitement and all and I think I shoved it somewhere out of sight, just to get it out of the way."

"Box?"

"Don't you remember? The box you picked up in the hall outside of Lenny's room before you rescued me. It had a, a sweater in it."

"Oh, sure. But I gave it to you. I haven't seen it since."

"That's just it, Mrs. Jacobson. I'm sure I left it in your living room while the police were questioning me."

"I don't think so."

"Yes. It's probably under a table. Ah, yes, there it is."

He reached under Mrs. Jacobson's table with one hand, holding his cup of tea in the other. He felt the box. Then he raised the drape and looked under it. The old dame didn't vacuum very much, thank God. There were huge balls of whitish dust around Old William Trevor Coxe's manuscript right where he had left it, still secured safe and sound with rubber bands. He put the box on his lap, using it as a tray for his teacup. There was some small talk about Lenny's funeral; they finished their tea, and then he tucked the manuscript under his arm, politely thanked her for the tea, and retraced that circuitous route to Fourth Avenue, which somehow seemed to be a place of sanctuary. He was unlocking the door to 80½ when he saw old Jacob Bluestein waving his crutch at him from across the street. He dodged the traffic and went over.

"Listen, Sonny. It's terrible about Lenny and all. I saw it on my television." He dabbed at his brow with a frayed handkerchief. "And the police have been here twice to ask me questions. Not only about Lenny but about you. What's going on? You can tell me. I'm Jacob Bluestein. Friend of your father's. Why was Lenny killed? Who did it? One of those Puerto Ricans moving in uptown? Listen, Howard, that Irish flatfoot. Mulvey, he said his name was. You know, he found four thousand dollars in hundreds rolled up in a sock in Lenny's room. That's a fortune! *Four thousand dollars!* Now where would a kid like Lenny get four grand unless he was mixed up in something he shouldna been? Howard, answer me!"

Lots of things were going through Howard's mind all at once. Larch hadn't stolen the money. Obviously, he hadn't been able to find it. He didn't have the manuscript, either. And he probably wanted both!

"Jacob, Jacob," he finally said. "You know Fourth Avenue book dealers never give away anything. Especially their secrets."

"What you mean, sonny boy?"

"I mean, how would I know where Lenny got the money? Why should he tell me?"

"Because you knew him best! I gotta feeling there's a lot you ain't telling, and Lenny Gould dead and not even buried. Good Jewish boy should be in the ground already. Somebody should be saying kaddish."

"They have to do an autopsy before the cops can release Lenny's body."

"Howard, I been talking to Walter Goldwater and Wolfgang Gottesman and Peter Stammer and Jack Tannen and Jack Biblo and Ben Bass and some of the other boys with the Fourth Avenue Booksellers Association. They're talking about trying to do something for Lenny. Taking up a collection."

"Jacob, that'll help. I already reached old man Butterman at the funeral home. Butterman used to buy books from my old man when they weren't playing chess. He's going to bury Lenny at cost. I'll let you know when the arrangements are made."

"That girl, the one who works at the library. Have you—"

"Yeah, I've talked to her on the phone. I'm going to see her tonight."

"But, about Lenny—"

"Jacob, no shit. I don't know anything. I'm trying to help the cops to find the guy who did this. Now look, I gotta scram. Got things to do. Gotta get back to the shop and feed Brummell and do a little business."

"You're getting too big for your britches, sonny. Your old man wasn't like that. *A little business!* You sound like them interior decorators uptown!"

Fourth Avenue's ultimate insult. Interior decorators were ritzy dealers who specialized in selling books in sets. Fancy leather editions that all looked alike and that nobody ever read, books arranged to be part of the decor of a room. The books might as well have been welded shut.

Jacob Bluestein was shaking his head and muttering and waving his crutch as Howard ran through the traffic and went inside 80½, locking the door behind him and leaving the CLOSED sign where it was.

He settled on the stool behind the counter and reached underneath to get the bottle of Dewar's when he remembered. The bottle was still at Lenny's. Empty. Knocked to the floor. Another victim of Richard James Larch. His hand felt a second bottle, a smaller one. It was a pint of apricot brandy, half-full. What the hell. He blew the dust off the bottle, removed the cap, and took a slug. He put the box containing the Coxe manuscript on the counter and thought about it for a while. Lenny's death was obviously the result of that manuscript, something Howard had put his whole fortune into and that he wasn't even sure he could sell.

He slipped the rubber bands off the box, took out the manuscript, and opened a page, then another, and started reading, slowly. Coxe it seems was in the middle of an insurrection in which an army officer by the name of Garantot was trying to beat off an angry mob that had surrounded an army barracks.

He sprang from the step on which he stood [Coxe wrote] and seized the most outspoken of the mob by the throat and cried out, "retreat villian, or you are a dead man." Among the plunderers were many soldiers belonging to different regiments, disguised like workmen. Garantot's troops murmured, refused to obey their leader, and swore they would not fire upon the people. The pillage was accordingly completed, and the soldiers, who laughed and diverted themselves with the event, permitted the rioters to pass quietly along with the stolen moveables. Garantot discharged a pistol but his regiment capitulated, and delivered up the unfortunate officer, who was torn in pieces, and his remains afterwards carried in triumph through the city. It is pretended that a woman, or rather a fury, devoured his heart. Throughout the whole kingdom the insurrections followed exactly the same course.

He sipped some more of the sweetish, foul-tasting brandy and read on. Apparently, troops of the monarchy tried to quell the uprising with a tough response.

One hundred and eighty-seven men and thirty-nine women were secured. Their captors took care not to confine them in the public prison, which might have been forced. A coach house, stable, and wood houses were ordered emptied, and prisoners were bound and shut in with a guard of fifty soldiers and an equal number of citizens over them. The two ringleaders were hanged; they had been robbers on the highway. Ten were whipped, branded, and sent to the gallies at Brest. All the rest were banished, and after a minute search in the quarries, two hundred and fifty more of a suspicious description were included in the sentence. Four women were also whipped, branded, and conveyed to the house of correction. If the other commanding officers had displayed the same firmness, and judgment in all the towns through the Kingdom, the people would have remained every where masters of the populace, and the revolution would have been a simple regeneration of the monarchy.

He wasn't sure what old Coxe was trying to tell him. But one thing he was positive about. Old Coxe was a law-and-order man. With a lot of strong opinions about France and the people who ran it at the time.

It may be fairly asserted that the kings of France have always supported their authority in an arbitrary manner. Louis XIII or rather his prime minister, the cardinal de Richelieu, governed by terror; Louis XVI by dignity; Louis XV, after a brilliant reign until 1748, dwindled into contempt.

Coxe went on and on but Howard's brain was too muddled to understand it all. Was there some fact or information in the document that made it important enough for Larch to kill to get it?

Or was it just the money? People murdered for less than that. A dime. A nickel. A smile. A frown. A word. Poor Lenny. Howard thought of Old Harry. What would he say about it all? He fumbled in the inside pocket of his jacket. It was still there. Harry's address and phone number. Like Coxe, Harry had powerful opinions about crime. So did Howard's old man.

"Penology," Harry said to Pop, "is in the hands of sentimentalists. They have turned dungeons and bull pens of the law into Y.M.C.A. camps. And the criminal, showing the slightest sign of piety, is delivered from his cage, almost with apologies."

"Christ," Pop said. "There is such a thing as forgiveness and redemption in the world, Harry. You want to go back to the day when they cut off fingers and ears and hanged women as witches?"

"You utterly miss the point, my bibliographic friend. Today's auto thief is nothing more than a deliberate, habitual, incurable criminal. Neither tethering him to a ball or chain nor slapping his hands with a ruler will ever cure him. When he is caught and jailed, it is, to him, merely the fortunes of war, the cost of doing business. As soon as he pays his debt to society, he resumes the practice of his profession."

"Oh yeah? What if it's some kid picked up after a joyride in a Studebaker? Is he your incurable criminal?"

"We are talking specifically about the degenerate, the thief who quits only when his eyes become dim or his legs arthritic. The punishments of old deserve to be restored: branding, whipping, dunking, forfeiture of goods. Why not ship our felons to some deserted islands of the Caribbean? By God, that's how Australia was settled by the British. Maryland and part of Virginia, too, for that matter."

"Harry, this is the twentieth century. It's about goddamned time you joined it. Society has gotta start showing compassion. No amount of punishment ever deterred a criminal, I can tell you that. We've got the death penalty on the books in all forty-eight states and it hasn't stopped murder."

"That is a common argument, as well as the one that gassing or frying or stringing up a man is disgusting, revolting business, and degrading to everyone who has to watch it. Indeed, many jobs are unpleasant, the garbageman's, the plumber's, the street sweeper's, and no less the hangman's. Deterrence is one of the aims of punishment but that's not the only one. Revenge is another. But still a better one is catharsis."

"What?"

"Catharsis. That's spelled c-a-t-h-a-r-s-i-s."

"I know how it's spelled, dammit. I just didn't know what you meant."

"I mean a salubrious discharge of emotions, a way of letting off steam. To hang a criminal, a murderer, let us say, produces immediate and grateful relief to the family of the victim, not to mention the same sense of satisfaction to decent but timorous men."

"Oh, shit, Harry, you can't go around hanging people just because it makes some of us feel good. Have you ever seen a hanging?"

"My dear sir, I have witnessed no fewer than nine hangings in my capacity as a journalist."

"And it made you feel good to watch somebody die in agony?"

"I felt no particular emotion. Hanging, if competently carried out, is quite humane, though perhaps not quite as quick as the electric chair and not as bloody as the firing squad. It seldom causes any physical or mental anguish. When the criminal reaches the end of his rope, it's much like a blow on the head with an ax."

"Your problem is," Pop roared, "is that people disgust you! You hold them with such contempt that their lives don't mean anything to you. You can watch nine men go to the gallows and call it humane."

"Not men, sir, criminals. Professional criminals. Every gunman should be strapped to the electric chair as soon as he fires his first shot, whether that shot kills or not. Because eventually it will kill."

And on and on, with Harry and Howard's old man yelling at each other and banging the counter until Pop pulled out the Dewar's.

"You are rigid, Harry," Pop lisped as the warmth of the whiskey began to envelop his chest.

"It is probably a psychological impossibility to convert me," Harry said. "It has never been achieved by anyone. Further, I dislike and distrust anyone who has changed his basic notions. When someone tells me that somehow I have shown him the light of day and cured him of his former wrongs, I am disgusted. I despise all Calvinists and communists, but I despise ex-Calvinists and ex-communists even more."

Maybe that's why Harry liked Howard's old man in spite of their violent disagreements. Not only was Pop not a Calvinist or a communist, he was as rigid as Harry. As far as Howard knew, Pop never changed his mind once in seventy-nine years. Pop wasn't around anymore. Howard couldn't get advice from him. But Harry was.

He closed the Coxe manuscript and put it back into its box, snapping the rubber bands around it. It had to be hidden, which wouldn't be hard in the clutter of 80½. He remembered a loose board in the floor back where the *National Geographic*s were stacked. He knelt and began pushing aside the magazines, with their cover stories of Australian aborigines, Tahitian natives, Eskimos, Laplanders, Mau Maus, Amazonian headhunters, Welsh coal miners, and Navaho Indians. Brummell the Cat peeked around a stack of books and swiped at him with his claw. Damned cat was most displeased. Howard hadn't fed him all day or the day before yesterday for that matter. The feline was tired of hunting for roaches and spiders and an occasional mouse.

Howard easily pried up a two-foot length of warped floorboard, which looked as though it had been laid down as an afterthought to fill in a gap in the floor caused by a nineteenth-century shortage of planks or something. He could see into the basement through the slits of the boards resting on the beams. He was aware of the glow from a light bulb that he knew burned night and day below. 80½ didn't have access to the cellar. The stairs to it were in old man Mandelblatt's bookstore next door. Mandelblatt paid a pretty penny to Klein the landlord for the use of the basement to store books. By cocking the box with the manuscript slightly, he eased it into the crack and laid it on the wooden slats. Then he returned the floorboard and stacked the *National Geographic*s back on top. It would take a while before anyone uncovered *An Englishman's Account of the Revolution of 1789 and the Taking of the Bastille.*

11

Ann Elkin and Howard sat across from each other holding hands over the Formica table on which she worked on her novel each night.

"A horrible experience for you, Howard. And poor Lenny . . ."

"Yeah. I never thought he'd end up that way."

"I still don't know why you didn't tell the police about the manuscript. You're convinced that's why Lenny was murdered by that thug Larch."

"I couldn't, that's all. It's supposed to be my ticket to the Cross Winds Hotel."

"And not telling them about your real relationship with Lenny . . ."

"Ann, it was an oath to my old man. And it means a lot to me that you didn't blab to the cops."

"But you can't hide all this forever. Jacob Bluestein told you the police found the money you gave Lenny to buy the manuscript. That means that the woman who sold it to him hasn't been paid. She's bound to come forward. Assuming there is such a woman! Frankly, I think Lenny stole that manuscript. Either from her or from a library or college. And that he and Larch were in it together somehow and had a disagreement."

"Where would Lenny have stolen it from? You read all the library journals. Was it ever reported stolen?"

"No."

"And Ronald Newberry told me it had been in private hands but missing for many years. Lenny would never have fallen in with someone like Larch. I'm *sure* he got it from that old lady." He pulled his hand from Ann's and snapped his fingers. "We can find out!"

"How?"

"We'll go talk to her."

Ann got up and went to the Frigidaire. She poured them each a glass of milk.

"And you know who she is?" Ann asked.

"I know *where* she is. Lenny told me she lives somewhere on Riverside Drive. One hundreth Street about."

"And you're just going to barge into someone's apartment and say, 'Hi, I'm Howard, I have your manuscript and the police have your money.'"

"Whitten."

"What?"

"I just remembered. Ronald Newberry told us that the manuscript was once in the hands of someone named Whitten." He snapped his fingers again. "The phone book. Get me the Manhattan phone book."

Ann got it from where she kept it under the sink and threw it with a thump onto the table. He opened the phone book and thumbed his way through the W's.

"Aha! I thought so."

"You found it?"

"There's a G. Whitten on page fifteen hundred thirty. And guess where G. Whitten lives?"

"Riverside Drive."

He sat back in his hard chair, a smile of satisfaction on his face. "See, this detective work isn't so tough."

"Tell the police about it, Howard."

"Never."

"Howard, do you know what you can get for withholding evidence?"

"No, what?"

"I don't know. But probably not less than five years in Sing Sing. Besides, something tells me that if G. Whitten is the old lady in question, you won't have to go to her. She'll be looking for *you*. To get her manuscript back. She'll have her lawyers on you. Eventually, she's going to find out that Lenny's dead, her manuscript's gone, the cops have her money, and that *you're* right in the middle of it all."

He sipped his milk.

"Ann," he said, "I don't think she's going to go to the police or anyone else. Lenny told me she's practically senile, heading for the old folk's home. On death's door."

"Then why bother to look for her at all, Howard? You're just asking for trouble."

"Two reasons. Now that Lenny's dead, she can vouch for the authenticity of the Coxe manuscript. Second, she can prove Lenny didn't steal it, that he bought it from her. Or was about to. She can get the money Lenny was going to give her from the cops. But I'm not going to let her know that I have the manuscript."

"There's no way you can talk to her without making her suspicious. What if everything falls apart? You'll end up having to give up the manuscript after all you've been through."

"Then maybe I can get my money back from the police somehow."

"How?"

"I *am* Lenny's only living relative, you know. I'm entitled to his estate."

"Shit, Howard! You can't prove the money was yours and you can't even prove you were related to Lenny."

"But—"

"There is no evidence that you are Lenny's half-brother."

"Pop said—"

"Forget Pop. He's dead. Lenny's mom is dead. Lenny's dead. To the police, you were just one of Lenny's acquaintances. You hired him part-time. Nothing else. For you, that four thousand dollars is gone. Forever. All you have now is the manuscript. And if you're not careful, you're not going to have that very much longer. Christ, Howard, didn't I tell you not to get involved with Lenny in this thing?"

"What's the use of talking about that now, Ann? You know what I've been through and you're giving me enough shit to last for years!"

Ann plunked down her glass of milk. Hard.

"Dammit, Howard, if you don't want to listen to what I say, then leave. Just leave! I have work to do."

"Ann . . ." he reached for her hand.

"No," she said, standing up. "I want you to go. I must get back to my work. Edgar Ardery is putting the pressure on me. Helen and Alexander are waiting in ancient Greece."

Chirpy the Canary flew to her shoulder and looked at Howard defiantly, its eyes darting, beak moving, taking its stand with Ann. Vicious bird.

"Ann, go look at those lions outside the library again and tell me what their names are."

"Howard, fuck you."

Fifty-first Street seemed quieter than usual as he turned away from Ann's brownstone. It had rained lightly a bit earlier and the sidewalks were still damp, giving off an odor of concrete and leather. He thought he heard footsteps behind him but when he turned, there was no one but a decrepit old woman wearing layers of clothing poking through a garbage pail. Ann hated him, he thought. Jacob Bluestein hated him. He almost hated himself. Things had gotten too complicated for a guy who never finished Evander Childs High School and who until now had been content to plan his limited future from a dusty store on Fourth Avenue. He had Lenny to bury. A manuscript to sell. And the cops had a killer on the loose.

12

"I guess you're wondering why I called you here, Mr. Howard."

"Sergeant, Howard's my fi—"

"Why don't you sit down over there?"

Mulvey buttoned his double-breasted suit coat. A toothpick protruded from the corner of his mouth.

Howard sank into Ronald Newberry's leather sofa, his hand lightly rubbing its cool texture. Newberry and Miss Kelly stood side by side like skinny Tweedledees and Tweedledums next to the Queen Anne table.

"I wasn't too surprised when you phoned me," Howard heard himself saying. "Obviously about Lenny. The murder."

"Right. During the course of our investigation, we discovered that the victim had done some work for Mr. Newberry."

"Ah, very minor work, Sergeant," Newberry said. "Mainly running errands and the like during auctions."

"Check. Now Mr. Howard, Mr. Newberry and Miss Kelly here told us that you and the deceased paid a visit to the gallery not long before the killing."

"Yeah."

"Why didn't you tell us about that, Mr. Howard?"

"I forgot about it. I can't remember everywhere I been with Lenny. We had chop suey in Chinatown a few days before and I didn't tell you about that, either."

Mulvey took the toothpick from his mouth and put it in the breast pocket of his baggy suit to be used again. Then he produced a pack of Luckies and offered one to Newberry. The dealer shook his head and instead removed a gold cigarette pack from his inside breast pocket and passed a Gauloise to Miss Kelly before lighting one for himself. No one offered Howard anything. Howard was sure that the cop thought he was some kind of crook and that Newberry thought he was a bum. Maybe they were both right.

"It seems like to me," Mulvey said, "that your visit here had more than the usual significance." He dragged on the cigarette. "Mr. Newberry here tells me that you and Mr. Gould indicated an interest in original manuscripts."

"Ah, it was *Lenny* that was interested."

"Don't you find it at all unusual, Mr. Howard? Your claim that you were attacked by a man wanted as a notorious thief of rare books and *manuscripts?*"

"You've decided that Lenny was mixed up with this Larch?"

"I'm not saying that at all. But it does seem to be reasonable that Lenny Gould's perpetrator was not some casual killer but someone involved with Mr. Gould in some way. It's possible that Mr. Gould had something, perhaps a rare book or manuscript, that Larch wanted. What do you think, Mr. Howard?"

Howard tried to figure a way not to tell the truth without actually lying.

"As far as I know, Sergeant Mulvey, Lenny didn't have in his possession any kind of rare manuscript or book at the time he was killed."

"And yet, we found a balled-up sock containing four thousand dollars in Mr. Gould's apartment. *Four thousand dollars!* A near fortune to someone like your late friend. Can you account for that?"

"Lenny must have saved it up."

"Yeah, sure. Do you think someone may have found out that Lenny Gould had all that money and murdered him for it but lammed without finding the loot?" Howard looked at Newberry and Kelly. They looked back at him. Mulvey paced the room. "How about this? What if Mr. Gould had a valuable book or manuscript and the killer went to him with the money to buy it. There was an argument. Lenny Gould was murdered. Then the killer dropped the money and escaped when you arrived."

Mulvey stood by a mahogany table and began to absently thumb through a manuscript. It looked like one of Newberry's George Washington originals. An ash grew longer on the tip of Mulvey's cigarette. Howard kept waiting for it to drop onto the document. Newberry stood there tense, also anticipating its fall. Mulvey turned sharply and the ash fell, some of it to the floor and some on the knee of Mulvey's trousers. The detective didn't notice. A relieved Newberry sighed. Interior decorators didn't like to see Lucky Strikes burn holes into $20,000 manuscripts.

"Now you, Mr. Newberry," Mulvey said, "did Mr. Gould indicate to you an interest in any *specific* manuscript?"

Newberry dragged on his cigarette. "Well, we discussed a number of documents that afternoon. I mean, there were several Washingtons we looked at. I remember we talked about *Tamerlane*."

"*Tamerlane?*"

"Poe's first book. But, no, I can't seem to recall anything specific other than those items. Perhaps, Miss Kelly—"

"I wasn't in the room for much of the discussion," the woman said. She exhaled her Gauloise and closed her eyes as the smoke surrounded her bony face.

"I'm still looking for a motive," Mulvey said.

"Perhaps, I can help you, Sergeant," Newberry said. "You told me that Mr. Howard here had never actually seen this man Larch before. So perhaps it was *not* Larch who committed the murder at all but some wino or cocaine addict or someone high on reefer. After all, Lenny Gould lived in a neighborhood that is changing from Irish and Jewish and Italian to Spanish. The area is, ah, becoming less desirable. The ransacking of his apartment was probably the result of a casual break-in."

"I haven't completely ruled that theory out," Mulvey said. "But there are just too many unanswered questions to suit me." Mulvey did a little more pacing. "Tell me, Mr. Newberry, you been in books and manuscripts for some time. I see you've even written a book on collecting." He scratched his head. Little flakes of dandruff fell to his shoulder. "I don't quite understand your racket. Why would anyone want to go out and spend a lot of money for a book when you can check one out of the library for nothing?"

Newberry expanded. He was used to patronizing fools. He wasn't going to spare Mulvey. One of Newberry's eyes seemed to look at Howard, the other at the cop.

"My dear Sergeant, the lure of collecting has its roots in the chase, not for survival but for the sport. And the bigger and more dangerous the quarry, the better—the difference between the quest for an elephant and the hunt for a squirrel. Surely you, too, must have collected something in your youth."

"Stamps. I had a stamp collection."

"Philately."

"No, stamps."

"As you say, Sergeant. The hobby of Franklin Roosevelt and King George the Fifth and King George the Sixth. And no doubt you felt the delight of owning and touching your collection."

"I always wanted that stamp, you know, the one with the upside-down plane on it.

"Very rare."

"Marbles."

"What?"

"I also collected marbles. Aggies."

"Now you're getting the idea, Sergeant. Butterflies, rocks, sea-shells, art. *Anything* can be collected. But books! Manuscripts! They add a higher dimension, one of the intellect. Books immortalize all forms of human endeavor, whether it is man's literature and art or science and discovery."

Mulvey reached for a copy of Newberry's book, *Collecting the Rare and the Beautiful,* and leafed through it as Newberry spoke.

"Jonathan Swift wrote that 'books are children of the brain.' " And it was Richard Addison who said, 'Books are the legacies that a great genius leaves to mankind.' And Carlyle: 'In books lives the soul of the whole Past Time.' "

Mulvey interrupted, reading from Newberry's tome: " 'The authors of books are a natural and irresistible aristocracy [he stumbled when he came to the word *aristocracy*] in every society, and, more than kings or emperors, exert an influence on mankind.' That's in there, too."

"Quite," Newberry said. "That was Mr. Thoreau."

"So there must be a lot of money in supplying a special book to some swell who really wants it."

"Not just *any* book, Sergeant. *Any* book you can pick up on Fourth Avenue, as Mr. Howard here can attest. I provide people with the best in our history and our art. To people who can not only afford what I offer but who also adore it, love it, covet it."

Mulvey scratched his head. "I just wonder if any of those people you're talking about would kill for something they adore, love, and covet if they can't get it any other way."

"Sergeant, my clients are among the most sophisticated and refined segment of America, not violent monsters or penniless intellectuals scrounging through the garbage books of Fourth Avenue." Newberry turned to Howard. "Sorry, Mr. Howard, that was not meant as a personal affront."

"Howard's my f—"

Mulvey tossed Newberry's book with a thud onto a shiny, waxed table. Newberry grimaced when it hit.

"Well, Gentlemen. And Miss Kelly," Mulvey said. "I guess I get the idea. Not sure I understand it all, though. One more question, Mr. Newberry. You yourself never ran across this character Larch personally by any chance?"

"Don't be ridiculous, Sergeant. The man's a thief and an outlaw. No one in the bibliographic industry would have anything to do with with such a vagabond. No self-respecting member of the trade, I mean."

"Just thought I'd ask." Mulvey started toward the door. "Look, if anything comes to mind to any of you about a possible motive for Lenny Gould's death, I want you to call me. Just ask for Homicide at the two-three precinct. Upper East Side. Leave a message if I'm not there."

"I can go now, Sergeant?" Howard asked.

"Of course, pal. You're not exactly under arrest now, are you?"
Mulvey picked up Newberry's book on collecting from the table.
"Ah, Mr. Newberry, I'd kinda like to read this book. Maybe it'll
shed a little more light on your business. You got a spare copy?"

"It's for sale, Sergeant. One ninety-eight."

"One ninety-eight." Mulvey put the book back down. "Maybe
the library's got it."

13

Sweating, Howard took the number 6 train down to Union Square.
Damn that Mulvey, he thought as he looked at the picture of a
pretty girl in a Miss Rheingold beer ad. The cop talked like he was
on to something, but what? And Newberry! He either lied or really
did forget when he told Mulvey he couldn't remember which manuscript Lenny and Howard had asked him about. Hell, Newberry
even offered to buy it. Howard was sure that leather merchant
wouldn't have forgotten that. Bastard was up to something.

It was just about sundown on Fourth Avenue when he opened
the door to Jacob Bluestein's store and went in.

"Jacob."

"You!" The one-legged bookseller rose up in his seat by the door.

"I know you're still pissed, Jacob, but I came to tell you about
Lenny's funeral. You know I been making the arrangements."

Jacob relaxed a little.

"I should hope the hell you are, Sonny," he said. "You don't
want some flunky for that Tammany Hall hack O'Dwyer to bury
him and and dump him with all those other forgotten bastards on
Hart's Island."

"Of course not. Lenny was like, well, like family."

"Yeah, I guess you and your old man was the closest thing to kin that Lenny ever had. Almost like a father and a brother to him."

The bell at Bluestein's front door tinkled as a customer wearing a snap-brim hat came in and began browsing. They ignored him. Secondhand dealers always ignored customers unless they suspected them of shoplifting.

"Listen, Jacob, you told me you've been talking about Lenny with Gottesman and Goldwater and Bass and Tannen and Biblo and the rest from the Fourth Avenue Booksellers Association and they said something about taking up a collection. The service is going to be on Wednesday up at Butterman's on Amsterdam Avenue. We all gotta come up with a few bucks to help pay for it. Now I talked to old Butterman himself. He's willing to carry most of the funeral. You know, the casket and all and a hearse to go up to Woodlawn. But we've got to do something to help out. Since Lenny didn't have any relatives, I guess the city will get anything he has left, including that four grand. So everyone's gotta pitch in."

"We'll come up with something. Some folks around here didn't like Lenny all that much, though. And I know a lot of people here think Lenny should have been buried long before now. Like a good Jew."

"Lenny wasn't a good Jew, Jacob."

"Don't matter. Lot of folks on Fourth Avenue ain't good Jews, either. But when the chips are down, they go back to their Russian roots and do a little soul-searching. Try to make things right. But Lenny *was* one of us." Jacob hit an arthritic finger against an eye as if to dab away a tear. "You know, they say us book dealers are independent bastards and there's no doubt about that. But we all get shits when one of us goes out of business or retires South or has a heart attack or dies. There ain't *that* many of us and with this new television coming in and all and with radios and movies, some day there might even be fewer of us. There could even be a time when nobody buys secondhand books anymore and there's nothing left on Fourth Avenue but thrift stores and antique shops."

"That'll *never* happen, Jacob, Howard said. "The world needs books. And as long as it does, there'll always be a Fourth Avenue around to supply them."

"Say, excuse me." It was the customer, guy with a wooden matchstick in his mouth, who pushed his snap-brim hat at an angle on his head.

"You see we're talking?" Bluestein said.

"Yeah, I see but I gotta question." He was holding a book.

"Make it fast," Bluestein said.

"You gotta price of one dollar and fifty cents on this thing. Now look, that's a little steep. Binding's loose and all. How's about taking seventy-five cents?"

"Seventy-five cents?" Bluestein said. "Lemme see that book."

He took it from the man's hands and opened it up.

"You wanna buy it for seventy-five cents, huh? Seventy-five cents? How about this?" Bluestein ripped at the front and back covers with all his strength, pulling the book apart. Then he tore at the pages, ripping them out. Finally he wadded the whole mess together and threw it at the snap-brim's feet.

"You want it, Mister, buy it. Two dollars and fifty cents. No, make it four fifty. On second thought, you can't have it for nothing, Mister. Nothing, you hear? It ain't for sale. At any price. Now get the hell out of my store. I ain't sellin you nothing."

"But—"

"Out!"

Bluestein grabbed his crutch and began to raise it over his head.

The matchstick fell out of snap-brim's mouth. "Madman!" he shouted as he raced to the door and flung himself out onto Fourth Avenue.

"Guess I told that bastard a thing or two," muttered Bluestein, reaching under the counter for his bottle of Dewar's.

"But why, Jacob, why?" Howard asked. "You lost the sale, the book, *and* the customer?"

"I didn't like the looks of that guy. He was no reader anyway.

Guy didn't even know why he wanted that book. Bastard just wanted to make a deal, that's all. Wanted to Jew me down. Don't have to sell to nobody I don't like, and him I don't like."

Jacob poured himself a stiff one. Howard shook his head. "Jacob, listen. Wednesday. Eleven in the morning. At Butterman's. For Lenny."

He crossed around the traffic to 80½, where Brummell slapped at him with one paw and then with the other as soon as he walked in. The tumor on his head seemed to have grown. He must have been feeding it. Howard poured the animal some dried cat food. Then he decided. In spite of what Ann said, he was going uptown to find the old lady. Maybe she was blind and deaf and senile. But he needed to talk to her. Find out about the manuscript. In a way, he owed it to her. It wasn't that he intended to give it back. He wasn't that dumb. But he had to see her. There was a quarter of a pint of apricot brandy left and he drank it right out of the bottle and threw the empty onto a stack of *Life* magazines. Christ, he felt like getting drunk. Harry would have said full steam ahead. He never minded getting a little soused.

"I am ombibulous," Harry told Pop. He claimed to enjoy every known alcoholic drink. Although, he admitted that he liked beer the best. But only after he finished his work. "The intelligent man never picks up the jug until he concludes the important business before him, no matter whether manual or intellectual. Then the rational man may ease the tautness of his nerves and the tumor in his spleen by downing the elixir of inebriation. The most exhilarating and charming activities are performed by men who are, you might say, three sheets to the wind."

And there was hardly a time when Harry was in the store that he didn't rail at Pop about the Great Experiment, which the bookseller didn't think was any too great, either.

"But we have to obey the law," Pop said. "The Eighteenth Amendment was the law of the land. And even if it was insane, we had to go along with it because we live in a democracy and we follow the will of the people."

"My noble bookseller," Harry replied. "Do not allow me to characterize the yokels who tried to permanently parch our tonsils. I'm unsure why the Great Unwashed were granted the right to vote in the first place."

"It was still the law, Harry."

"The law! Do you know what it cost to enforce such madness in the forty-eight states? It cost fifty million dollars a year just to hire regiments of agents provocateurs, spies, detectives, informers, liars, and cheats to make sure the foam did not touch some innocent's lips. And twenty percent of liquor enforcers were corrupt. Then there was the half a billion dollars a year the states and the federal government lost in licenses and taxes from the commercial sale of the stuff."

"I agree it was stupid, Harry. But we're Americans and the majority rules."

"The majority created a law that was not equipped to deal with the army of bootleggers smuggling wines and liquors in from the Caribbean and Canada. The majority created a whole new gangster element, armed with machine guns. Even private citizens risked the wrath of Uncle Sam by brewing their own at home in the privacy of their bathtubs. Now, it was perfectly lawful to import wines for medicinal and sacramental purposes. That's why the bootleggers brought in champagne as medicine and the good Jewish rabbis of the Lower East Side of your very own city profited at the tune of fifteen dollars a case selling wine for rituals to Jews of good standing. Barbaric! And you, my bibliographic friend, have even admitted consuming such liquid from time to time during that disastrous decade."

"For rituals only, Harry. Rituals."

"No doubt you consumed a daily ritual to compensate for those bleak years. As for me, Prohibition or not, I never on a single occasion was unable to obtain a drink when I wanted one. Usually within ten minutes of arriving in a strange burg, I would have my foot up on the rail hoisting a tall, cold one. Only once did I have a close call. In Bethlehem, Pennsylvania, in 1924. I had gone there to hear the Bach Choir, for there could be no other reason I would have gone to Bethlehem, Pennsylvania. There was not a drop of brew to be had in the local hotels, the pubs, the restaurants, the speakeasies. I threw myself on the mercy of cabdrivers, the police, the fire department, the mayor, the Elks, even the clergy. But all reported that Prohibition agents had been spotted in the hills and every bartender was standing vigil. An hour before my train was to leave for New York, I decided to wire the city to have a bootlegger meet me in Paterson, New Jersey, to fortify me for the rest of the trip back. But on the way to the station in Bethlehem, I encountered a sympathetic cabbie who delivered me to a seafood house whose proprietor peeked through a crack in the door and demanded that I prove I was not a revenue agent. I insisted I was a musician, in Bethlehem to hear Bach and I produced the piano score of the B Minor Mass I had been carrying with me all the time. I consumed three Humpen and two sandwiches for forty-five cents and made my train just as it was pulling out. My thirst was quenched. I had saved myself from death. Thanks to Johann Sebastian Bach."

Harry shook his head sadly but with a little smile as he recalled his triumph.

"My friend, I shall never forget one of the most important dates of my life. Midnight. April 6, 1933. I stood at the bar of the Hotel Rennert in Baltimore and hoisted a foamy glass to my lips, my first legal taste of beer since those cow-state morons inflicted the nightmare on us nearly thirteen years before. Imagine, those ciphers, those blanks out in Iowa and Kansas, those crackers in Georgia and Mississippi, abandoning their cattle and their cotton to peak into the windows of my home and tell me what I may or may not drink with my meals, as if they have a right, nay, a sacred duty to do so."

"Harry, nobody says the law's always right."

"The law is never right! Some semi-illiterate preacher in Boston tries to tell me what I may read. Some ignorant bureaucrat in Washington, inspired by God, determines what I may receive in the mail. I may not buy lottery tickets because it offends the dung-kickers out in Oklahoma. I must keep Sunday as the Sabbath because there are assholes who believe that Genesis cannot be wrong. So it goes, my bookselling friend. Those are the laws we have in the greatest of the free nations."

Ah, Harry. So much anger. So much truth.

"Never believe a clergyman," Harry cautioned Pop, lighting up an Uncle Willie, puffing madly, his eyes bulging, his nostrils flaring. "A clergyman makes his living assuring idiots he can save them from an imaginary hell. In the same way, a midway snake-oil salesman assures the clodhoppers who listen to him that he can save them from baldness. These are the people who would stop our drink at the point of a gun. They are purveyors of theological hocus-pocus who would be better off practicing their stuff in the Congo than in twentieth-century America."

"Theological hocus-pocus my ass!" Pop screamed. "You have no faith, no trust in a higher wisdom, no belief in a greater power. But it happens to be a fact that all humans need the security of believing that there's someone up there watching and protecting them. Whether or not there is!"

"Nonsense!"

"Harry, you oughta head for the nearest church or synagogue and pray for forgiveness."

"The nearest church or synagogue? Certainly there are better and more profound uses for the real estate on which they stand. Colleges could be built on the site of churches, for example. Or schools. Or taverns where men of good fellowship share their intellect. Music halls where good German music shakes the rafters. Sporting clubs. By that I mean cathouses. And there must be more useful occupations for ex-clergymen than banging Bibles on pulpits. Arm them with brooms, and they are far less dangerous and more productive than with Bibles behind a podium."

Pop voiced his rage and then he and Harry drank a few rituals.

14

He was armed with a name and an address. G. Whitten. Two hundred seventy-eight Riverside Drive. The number 2 train took him to Ninety-sixth and Broadway. Then he walked over to the service road along Riverside Drive, up to the Firemen's Memorial at the end of West 100th Street. It was nearly dusk, a time when he knew most everyone would be in. Huge brick buildings lined the drive and hundreds of brownstones sat side by side on the side streets. He imagined the faces of elderly widows who were staring vacantly over the Hudson River in lonely wait from behind the windows of those grand old apartment houses. He only needed to find one old lady.

He was nervous as he went to the doorman. But he was prepared with a cover story and he carried a briefcase.

"Excuse me," he said.

"Yes sir. Who do you want to see?"

The doorman was wearing a blue uniform with lots of buttons and a heavily braided cap. With a sword and scabbard, he might have passed for an admiral in the Turkish Navy.

"I know I got the right building," Howard said, "but the name of the party I'm looking for has slipped my mind. A Mrs. . . . Mrs. Oh, Christ, you know the one. Old lady. The widow. I'm her insurance man. She wants to see me tonight."

"We've got several old ladies in this building, Mister. Maybe you'd better go back to your office and get her name."

"Oh, the office's closed at this hour. Here's my card." Howard handed him a business card that some insurance agent had forced on him a few weeks before.

"She wanted to see me right away because she's old and she's getting her affairs in order, so I came right up. I guess I was stupid to have forgotten to write her name down—but I did remember the address. You know how hectic things can get when you're in a hurry."

The doorman handed the card back.

"Really can't help you, Mr. Snyder. We've got a number of widows here."

"But you must know the one I'm talking about. Woman has a big collection of books and manuscripts. Her late husband or father or grandfather or somebody was a collector."

"Naw, don't think . . . Wait, there is Mrs. Steinberg in Sixteen-F. She's old and a widow and I know she has a lot of books."

"Steinberg?"

"Always reading. Always carrying a book when she goes out."

"That doesn't sound like the one."

"She likes to read in the park."

"I don't think—"

"But she ain't here. She's visiting her sister in Arizona. She's been there for two months."

"Oh."

"Course there is Mrs. Esterhazy in Four-B. She was telling me the other day about some book she was reading, something by Pearl Buck. So she's got books. And she's old."

"Mrs. Esterhazy."

"But she ain't home, either. She went to see *Brigadoon* with Mrs. Umhoefer in Eleven-A. Mrs. Umhoefer's also a widow but I know for a fact she doesn't do any reading because of her cataracts. Listens to the radio a lot. She was telling me her favorite show's "Break the Bank" with Bert Parks. Quiz-show junk. Some people will listen to anything. Me, I go for action. You hear "Casy Crime Photographer," the other night? You know, the one with Stats Cotsworth. That's what I always wanted to be. A photographer for *The Daily News*. I'm a news buff. Winchell, Murrow, Davis, Shirer, Kaltenborn. I listen to them all."

Howard was getting impatient.

"Wait, wait," he said. "The name of the woman I'm supposed to see. I just remembered. It's Whitten."

"Oh, Whitten. Sure, Mrs. Gertrude Whitten. Now, I know for a fact she had a lot of books. A hell of a lot." He pulled a Milky Way from his tunic, opened it, and bit into it thoughtfully. "They were old books, too. Guy from a bookstore came up in a station wagon and hauled them out. Just yesterday. Didn't waste no time, either. She'd only been dead a couple of days. Bad heart. And they're cleaning out her stuff already. You can blame her son-in-law for that. Greedy bastard. Think he ever left me a tip when I flagged down a cab for him? No way."

"You say a guy from a bookstore came and hauled out her books?"

"Yeah, who else would want them?"

"You don't know his name do you?"

"Son-in-law? Sure, Liebknecht. Think he's a doctor over at Mount Sinai. Damned tightwad. Hate doctors."

"No, no, I mean the book dealer. Do you know the name of the guy who picked up her books?

"Shit, Mister. How would I know? This is a big building. People come in here all the time making deliveries and picking things up. I don't ask their names."

"Damn," Howard said. "Thanks anyway."

"But I can tell you something funny about that book guy." The doorman bit into his Milky Way again and chewed some more, taking his time. "He had these funny eyes. Couldn't tell which one was looking at you. Threw me off a little. But he gave me two bucks for holding the door open for him while he and this woman he came with loaded up his station wagon. Can't get over those funny eyes."

Howard wandered into the park. Looking behind him, he could see that most of the lights were on in the big apartment buildings on Riverside Drive. The lights seemed to flash secret messages across the Hudson. He sank onto a park bench. Lenny hadn't lied. One hundreth and Riverside. Pay dirt. Poor Mrs. Whitten. Dead. Bad heart. Her books gone. Now obviously in the hands of Ronald Newberry and Miss Kelly. All except the William Trevor Coxe manuscript and Howard had it. First Lenny. Then Mrs. Whitten.

She was an old lady. How could the doorman know she died of a heart attack? A frail, old lady. Fragile. Someone could have put a pillow over her head. It might look like heart failure. They'd never do an autopsy. That monster Larch. He could have done it. Killed her just like he did Lenny.

Things had gone too far. Maybe Ann was right. Maybe he should call Mulvey at the Twenty-third Precinct. Confess. Give up the Coxe manuscript. Maybe the penalty for concealing evidence wasn't all that bad. Maybe . . .

He felt a heavy hand around his throat.

"*I gotta talk to you. Don't move!*"

Howard's body jerked involuntarily.

"I said don't move!"

His breath was steamy at the back of Howard's neck. He needed Listerine. It was Larch. In the park.

"Larch!" Howard managed to choke out the words despite the pressure on his throat. "Don't kill me. Please!"

"I need something from you."

Howard struggled against the weight on his neck but he was pinned against the bench. He heard a bell. Bells. Chimes. Heavenly chimes. Pop, Lenny, he thought, I'm coming! I'm joining you in those dusty book stacks up there or down there, wherever you are. I'm coming, Pop! I'll be there. Just don't give me inventory again.

"Watch out!" he heard a voice shout. It wasn't Larch's voice. Or Pop's or Lenny's. He felt a jolt. He felt Larch heave. The grip on his throat relaxed. Suddenly the weight was gone and he pitched forward onto the grass. He looked up and saw Larch entangled with a bicycle rider.

"Goddamn you!" Larch shouted as he tried to push the bike off of him.

"Hey, Mister," said the kid who had been on the two-wheeler, "it's almost dark. I didn't see you until too late. I rang my bell!" The kid was wrapped under the bike on top of Larch. Howard picked himself up and began running up the embankment toward Riverside Drive.

"Come back here!" shouted Larch. "Come back!" His voice became fainter as the distance between them became wider. Howard was almost clipped by a Chevy whose driver honked angrily as he ran across the roadway. He got to West End Avenue at Ninety-seventh Street, then over to Broadway, which was crowded with window-shoppers. An all-night newsstand stood at Ninety-sixth Street and an express subway stop. There was safety in numbers and he vanished into the crowd. There was no question about it now. Larch the killer was loose and he wanted Howard and the manuscript.

Christ, what would Harry do?

15

"Friends, we are here to honor the memory of our departed colleague, Leonard Abraham Gould." He coughed. The speaker was Wolfgang Gottesman, who ran the Bright Star Book Store on Twelfth Street. Gottesman had fled Germany in the early 1930s after Hitler's thugs burned his store to the ground in Munich. He had known Lenny for as long as Howard and the rest, and everyone agreed Gottesman was the smartest man on Fourth Avenue.

Lenny lay in a closed casket in a small chamber of Butterman's Funeral Home on Amsterdam Avenue. There were several wreaths of flowers beside the simple wooden coffin. One was a colossal floral arrangement sent by Ronald Newberry who wasn't there. About a dozen people sat in folding chairs. There was Tannen and Mandelblatt. Bluestein and Bass. Biblo and Goldwater. Stammer was there, too. Mrs. Jacobson. And Klein the landlord. All the men wore hats out of respect. Only Wolfgang Gottesman wore a skull-cap. Ann Elkin was next to Howard, her shoulder against his. He had told her about his run-in with Larch and she was afraid for him.

Gottesman stood tall and gaunt. His black hair streaked by gray fell over his collar. Men didn't usually let their hair grow that long in 1948. His eyelids were heavy. There were dark furrows in his forehead and down the cheek lines. Gottesman was tired. Tired of running from assassins, tired of selling books for pennies, tired of death.

"Lenny Gould was born on September 11, 1927, at Mount Sinai Hospital in Manhattan to Shirley Glover Gould. He attended P.S. One twenty-one, graduated from the Bronx High School of Science, and was attending the City College of New York at the time of his . . ." Gottesman fumbled. "At the time of his death. Ever since Lenny was a teenager, he worked part-time on Fourth Avenue, helping to do what we all do there. Sell books. Lenny was truly a bookman."

There was a sob. Jacob Bluestein put a frayed handkerchief to his eyes. Then he blew his nose. Howard had never seen him so sentimental about Lenny, a kid Jacob used to describe as a loud-mouth little prick. A know-it-all. A pimply, four-eyed little bastard. Death changes attitudes. And Jacob had complained bitterly that there was no rabbi to conduct Lenny's services.

"Lenny also worked uptown at the Caesar Auction Galleries on Madison Avenue. He would go back to Fourth Avenue, telling us about Dickens in 'parts' and Scott in 'boards.' He knew about gilt, beveled edges, tooling. He could describe books that were folio, quarto, octavo, duodecimo. He knew rectos and versos. Lenny could tell you about buckram and vellum. How many of us here can say we ever knew what he was talking about?"

There was a murmur of agreement.

Gottesman coughed several times. "Lenny may have been the ultimate bibliophile. He used to say that he wanted to own one copy of every book ever printed, not an easy task for a kid who was going to college and who was always broke and who lived in one room. Lenny wasn't one who cared only about the tactile, visual aspects of books, the binding, the paper, the type. He also cared about what was inside. John Donne wrote, 'The world is a great volume and Man the Index of that Book.' Lenny knew that and he was aware that a library, simply a collection of books, is a garden needing perpetual cultivation. Lenny was a gardener, a cultivator."

Clunk!

Heads turned. Jacob Bluestein's crutch had slipped to the floor. He groped for it and put it in an upright position.

"To finish, let me say that Lenny was not a religious man, nor are many of us here this morning. Yet Lenny would probably approve of this passage from the Bible, the book of Job, in which it is written that, 'My desire is, that the Almighty would answer me, and that mine adversary had written a book.' "

Wolfgang Gottesman sat down. His head was bowed, the lines in his face etched even deeper.

There was silence for a bit, then Jacob Bluestein struggled to his foot with the aid of his crutch. Jacob had shaved that morning and was wearing what passed for his best suit, a shirt with a frayed collar that had once been white but that had yellowed with age, and a tie illustrated with a picture of Niagara Falls, almost as wide as the shirt. It was Jacob's dress tie.

He brushed away a tear. "I just wanna say that I think it's a damned shame that Lenny had to go the way he did. I think it stinks. And if I ever find out who done it to him, he's gonna get the end of my crutch!"

"Jacob," Howard hissed. "Not here."

"He was a good boy, that Lenny. A credit to Fourth Avenue." Jacob slumped back to his seat. Ann Elkin gripped Howard's hand—their first firm physical contact since their fight.

"A credit to Fourth Avenue!" Jacob shouted. He got up on his one leg again. "To Fourth Avenue!"

Oh, Christ! What was it Harry used to say about death?

"Once, I decided to look up death in the library," Harry told Howard's old man one day. "And you know, there's damned little written about it. Which shows that most of us, preoccupied as we are by that inevitable conclusion, have surrendered to our ignorance of it, capitulating to the everyday necessity of living."

"That's bad?" Pop said. "We should give up thinking about life in order to devote our lives to death? Crazy!"

"It is proper to consider man's role in the universe, my bibliochum. Well, let me tell you that after two weeks of research at the Enoch Pratt Free Library, I found what I was looking for. It was a text by a Dr. Alan Mendelbaum of the esteemed Johns Hopkins School of Medicine. Dr. Mendelbaum had written a book entitled *The Body of Man,* and in it he wrote something to the effect that death is acidosis, caused by the failure of the organism to maintain the alkalinity necessary for normal functioning. I cherish that description. Death, I conclude, is not unlike a bottle of Chateau Margaux, which once uncorked undergoes a destructive fermentation. Life is not a struggle against sin or capitalism or bootleggers but simply against hydrogen ions. The dying man is simply losing the struggle against the hydrogen ions."

"Hydrogen ions my ass, Harry!" Pop snorted. "Like I've told you before, there's a legitimate reason to believe in a higher power than ourselves. Man has always had that need. Now, I'm not saying I have that need, but most of us do."

"Not at all. Most of us are just dumbfounded by what we do not understand. Death is the greatest mystery of mankind. Despite the absence of important books on the subject, the contemplation of death has obsessed man throughout the centuries. Man has developed the notion that death is a mere transition to a higher plane of life, that death is an incentive to this way or that way of living, that death is a benign panacea for all human suffering. The fact of the matter, my bookish friend, is that death is the last and worst of all the practical jokes played upon us poor mortals by whatever gods we create. The worst thing about death is not that men die tragically, but that most of us die ridiculously. We do not die at great moments, swiftly, cleanly, decorously, with heroism and surrounded by high and beautiful words. No, we die of arteriosclerosis, diabetes, toxemia, tuberculosis, scarlet fever, carcinoma of the liver. A man does not depart quickly and brilliantly like a stroke of lightning. He fades by inches."

"Harry, you're so damned fatalistic. What about your own death?"

"My death will be like all the rest. Painful, probably, and as ridiculous as anyone else's. But, Christ, how I hope it is quick. I dread being incapacitated, losing my faculties, becoming a burden to others. Lying in a deep sleep but not dead. That must not happen to me. I will not allow it!"

"You can't think about things like that, Harry. Not when you're alive and well. It does no good."

"Well? What makes you think I'm well? While I don't appear to have a disability, I am convinced I suffered a slight stroke in 1939. The left side of my face was stiff. I couldn't raise my left arm. The doctors at Johns Hopkins Hospital pronounced me fit after a month. What little they know! I dread the onslaught of autumn. Hay fever. My temperature is on the rise. There is no doubt that in the heat of summer I will develop pneumonia. My stomach has been roaring for days. I fart every ten minutes."

Harry opened his jacket, displaying red suspenders, pulled a soda mint from an inside pocket, popped it into his mouth, and sighed in relief as the coolness inched down his esophagus.

"Harry, we all fart. I was on the number Four train the other day sitting next to the most beautiful woman I had ever seen. She was a blond goddess, an image of perfection, a creature with a delicate nose and tiny ears who should have been encapsulated and placed in a glass case at the Metropolitan Museum."

"So?"

"Harry, this goddess let loose with a fart that emptied the car. And I was right beside her. I heard it. I smelled it. I got off two stops before I had to."

"One is aware when he or she is flatulent and so, unfortunately, is everyone else. But we don't know precisely when we die. Long after our hearts have stopped beating and our lungs refuse to swell with the vanity of our species, there are obscure

and remote parts of us that somehow live on, properly uncon-
cerned about our central catastrophe. Why, there are doctors
who have cut out our vital parts and have kept them alive for
months in jars. We can see those parts pulsating, beating. Ourselves living on."

"Harry, you know I never agree with you. But you oughta write
some of this down. You might find some boob to swallow all this
shit."

"And what makes you think I haven't? Intelligent as you are,
my worthy but dusty retailer, hiding behind your racing form,
you might consider reading more of the books you sell, including
my own."

A caravan of two cars followed the hearse up to Woodlawn
Cemetery. The skies were gray. The trees had surrendered their
leaves to the cold. There was no marker on the grave into which
Lenny's coffin was lowered. Maybe they would be able to afford
a tombstone some day. They stood, shivering, around the hole in
the ground. No one said anything. It had all been said. Ann Elkin
continued to hold Howard's hand.

"I've been to enough funerals to say that I have palled of them,"
Harry said to Pop. "Trashy, tedious, indelicate. That's what they
are. What we need is a service free from the pious but unsupported
assertions that revolt our minds but that remain graceful and con-
soling. We have enough poets for the job, certainly. I propose that
they meet in some quiet roadhouse and draw up a ritual that would
be filled with lovely poetry, but absent of any pronouncement on
the subject of a future life. Can we not corral Frost and Sandburg
and Edna St. Vincent Millay to develop a libretto to salute the
departed, now immortal and gaseous? The poets should spit on
their hands and get to work at once!"

The Fourth Avenue merchants weren't poets but they almost
acted as though they were that day. Harry would have approved.
Ann and Howard walked with Wolfgang Gottesman, now stooped

and looking old, to the limo that was to take them back into Manhattan.

"This is it, Howard," Gottesman said. "I'm getting out."

"Out?"

"Quitting. Closing down. The Bright Star Book Store is about to become extinct."

Howard shook his head.

"You know what a nova is, Howard?"

"A nova?"

"It's a star that becomes a thousand times brighter and then gradually fades away. That's the way it is with the Bright Star Book Store."

"But you been running it for nearly fifteen years."

"And I ran a store in Munich for another twenty years before the Nazis came. Howard, my kids aren't interested. They're professional people. Morris is a lawyer; David's a C.P.A. They don't want to run some nickel-and-dime business. I'm not that well. I've got this cough. My lungs are bad. The landlord tells me he's doubling the rent. People don't buy as many books, don't read as much. There's all this radio and this new television. Even Jacob Bluestein's got a TV now. Never thought that'd happen. One day the interior decorators will take over and only sell books for display purposes, like watercolors. Dealers will disperse books by mail out of their bedrooms to the few people left who want to read. They're selling paperback books in drugstores and grocery stores and bus stations for a quarter! I tell you, there won't be any secondhand dealers left."

"Isn't gonna happen, Wolfgang. Folks need to buy books secondhand. How many people can afford two bucks for a best-seller? And who wants a shelfful of cheap paperbacks that fall apart everytime the humidity changes? You're wrong, Wolfgang, they're always gonna need us. You'll be making a big mistake if you close down."

"Will I, Howard? I tried to sell the business and all its inventory intact so it goes on being the Bright Star, but nobody wants it. The star's about to go out, Howard. I'm going to liquidate my inventory. Then Freida and I will be going down to the Jersey Shore to live.

Open a little card shop. No more booktores for me, Howard. No more." He coughed.

No one said anything else on the ride back to the city.

16

Ann Elkin and Howard sat in a corner booth at Longchamps on Madison Avenue. She was eating a club sandwich. He had no appetite and sipped a Schlitz, alternating with puffs on a Chesterfield.

"I haven't had the chance to tell you before, Howard, what with the funeral and everything else, but I've got some wonderful news."

She looked at him expectantly, waiting for him to prompt her.

"Yes?" he said.

"I've been to Macmillan about my book." Her head kind of bobbed, waiting for another prompt.

"And?"

"They love it!"

"They're going to publish it this time?"

"Well, it's going to take some more work, Howard." She bit into her sandwich. Some lettuce and a piece of tomato fell to her plate.

"You're talking about the version you've set in Greece at the time of Alexander, the one with the heroine named Helen."

She chewed for a few moments, then swallowed before she spoke. "Not exactly . . ."

"You mean you've gone back to Florentine Italy and the Medicis?"

"I haven't done that either, Howard."

"Well, what the hell have you done?"

"Howard, Edgar Ardery is being very supportive. And he's about the best editor Macmillan has." She put her hand on Howard's. "Edgar's already comparing me to Margaret Mitchell. He says that when I pull it off, I'll make a bigger fortune than Kathleen Winsor."

"So they want more changes."

"He doesn't think Alexander's Greece is quite right. He's talking about—"

"About?"

"California!"

"California?"

"Eighteen forty-eight. A hundred years ago. The Gold Rush. Sutter's Mill. The Argonauts. The Union Pacific Railroad. San Francisco. Barbary Coast." Her words came in a rush. "Did you know at the time of the Gold Rush women numbered just ten percent of the population? I'm naming my heroine Nell. She's a beautiful and courageous woman who runs a brothel but becomes one of the most powerful figures in San Francisco. She's torn between three lovers: a man born in poverty but who singlehandedly builds California's greatest bank; another, a ship's captain who battles pirates and puts down a mutiny; and the third, a heroic doctor who fights plague and pestilence. It'll have *everything!* Including the earthquake."

"The earthquake didn't happen until 1906. I know for a fact because I saw it in a *National Geographic*."

"So there might have been an *earlier* earthquake."

"Ann," he said, grabbing her hand. "Macmillan told you that your Florentine Italy novel had everything. They told you your Grecian novel had everything. Now they say your Gold Rush novel will have everything."

"Edgar Ardery loves my heroine!"

"She's the *same* one over and over. She just makes a reappearance in any century you want to re-create. The point is, you can't keep starting from scratch at the whim of some editor who won't even give you a few bucks on account."

"Edgar needs more of a finished product before Macmillan will go for an advance. Dammit! You could be more supportive, Howard. Hawksmith is on my ass at the library all day; I work at my Smith-Corona all night, and I don't get a goddamned word of encouragement from you." She took a lace hankie from her purse and daubed at her eye.

"I love you, Ann. Isn't that encouragement enough?"

He ordered another Schlitz. Ann had tea. They made up again. The conversation changed.

"Howard, this is serious. We've got to talk about it. After Larch attacked you in the park, you didn't do anything but run away. You've got to go to the police. You could have been killed!"

"I can't, Ann, you know that. They'll take away my manuscript. My whole life is invested in it."

"Your whole life? Howard, you could be dead right now. And what if that thing turns out to be worthless?"

"Dammit, I *know* it's authentic. I had Lenny's word for that."

"Howard, at least do this. Edgar says—"

"Edgar!" He spat the name.

"Yes, Edgar. He says he knows a professor at Columbia who's an expert on the French Revolution. He's done papers on Robespierre, Montesquieu, and Mirabeau."

"Whoever they are."

"Let him see the manuscript. Even if it is authentic, he can give you some idea of its historical value."

"I know what its historical value is."

"Oh, you big palooka!" She wiped at her eyes with her hankie again. "For the last time, call Detective Mulvey. You can't keep going on your own. You're going to get yourself killed."

"It's a chance I have to take."

"You're afraid for your life. You have to keep the manuscript hidden because you know it will be taken from you. With Lenny dead, you don't even know how to go about selling it. You can't keep going on like this!"

He looked into Ann's eyes.

"Your right," he said. "I *do* need advice."

"You'll call Mulvey, see that professor?"

"I mean *real* advice." He sipped his Schlitz, then put the glass down hard on the table. "Maybe I should go to Baltimore!"

"What's in Baltimore, for Christ's sake?"

He pulled out the slip of paper on which Harry had written his name and address.

"To see this guy." He pointed to the name on the paper. "He'd know what to do."

17

He stopped at Pennsylvania Station to pick up a timetable. Table 17 showed there were trains nearly every hour for the 185.5-mile run to Baltimore. He could catch one at Penn Station at 8:30 A.M., with stops in Trenton, Philadelphia, Wilmington, arriving in Baltimore at 11:48 A.M. The coach fare was $4.62 each way, $6.48 in a Pullman. He'd never ridden anything except coach.

It had taken him weeks to get up enough nerve to decide to go to Baltimore. And Lenny's murder was still unsolved.

That night, he slept in the store, armed with an old baseball bat, afraid to be too far away from his treasure. It was a fitful sleep because he could hear the rats scratching under the floorboards. He started with each sound. It could have been someone trying to break in. Uncomfortable. Two wooden folding chairs placed front to front. He curled up fetuslike on them and in the morning he was stiff, his joints aching. As the sun came up, he unlocked the front door and cautiously peeked outside. Fourth Avenue was all but empty, the storefronts quiet, waiting for their owners to launch a new day. A milk truck went by, the bottles rattling in their metal cages. No sign of Larch, no sign of the cops. He went back inside, where he shaved over the stained sink and anointed his hair with Kremil hair oil. Then he pulled the manuscript from its hiding place under the floor. Brummell clawed at him with an angry paw. He poured some tuna into the cat's bowl and gave him some water.

Then he heard the door rattle. Someone was trying to open it. Quickly, he put the box containing the manuscript under the counter and grabbed the baseball bat. He approached the door carefully and stood next to it. The knob rattled again. He heard a tapping on the window.

"Hello. Is anybody in there?" It was a woman's voice.

Tap. Tap. Tap.

Cautiously, he pulled the shade aside a crack and peeked out.

Miss Kelly.

He let the shade fall in place again and stepped back from the door, confused.

"Mr. Howard, I know you're in there. Please let me in."

He went back to the door and pulled the shade aside again, this time wider. It was Kelly all right. She was alone. He unlocked the door and opened it.

"Mr. Howard, I must talk to you. May I come in?"

"What's this all about?"

"We must talk privately."

"But—"

"Inside. "

He stood aside to let her in and then quickly closed and locked the door.

"I don't have much time, Miss Kelly—"

"Roberta. Call me Roberta."

"Roberta. You gotta scram. I have a train to catch."

"This won't take long. Do you mind?" She took out a silver cigarette case from the large black purse that dangled at her side and removed a Gauloise. He slapped his pockets for a matchbook, found one, and lighted her cigarette for her. Her face was angular, very thin, her blond hair long, emphasizing the leanness.

"I know you find it strange that I am here so early in the morning or that I'm here at all. Actually, I had been up to your room, in Washington Heights. No one was there, so I naturally thought that you might be here."

"You found me. Now what?"

"Did the floral arrangement for Mr. Gould arrive? At the funeral home?"

"Yeah."

"Naturally, Mr. Newberry and I were quite distressed by Mr. Gould's death. Ronald had his eye on that young man. Wanted to groom him for something better than, than—"

"Fourth Avenue?"

"Ronald believed that Mr. Gould had a future."

"Well, he didn't, did he?" He stood back and folded his arms. "Now just what is it you—"

"It's a proposition, Mr. Howard."

"Howard's my f—"

"Strictly a business proposition." Her neck arched, looking for an ashtray. There weren't any, so she flicked the ash from her Gauloise on the floor.

Brummell, his tumor shining, slinked from around a stack of *Collier's* and sniffed at the ash. Then he sat on his haunches and looked at Miss Kelly for a second before tearing at her with his paw. The claws snagged her leg.

"Oh, my nylon!" shouted Kelly, pulling her leg away from the cat.

"Brummell. Get the hell away!" Howard said. He picked up a battered copy of *Great Expectations* and flung it at him. Brummell sprang over the stack of *Collier's* and disappeared.

"Sorry, Miss Kelly. Brummell's not the friendliest cat on Fourth Avenue."

"So I see. That *beast* managed to cause a run in my stocking." She ran her long-nailed fingers down a thin leg.

"It's not that noticeable," he said. "You can barely see it."

"Enough of this! Let me tell you why I'm here." She pulled on her cigarette. "As you remember, you and Mr. Gould made it clear to us that you had access to a rare manuscript, a treatise on the French Revolution by William Trevor Coxe."

"We never admitted having it, Miss Kelly!"

"Roberta. Please, Mr. Howard, we're not stupid. It's not everyday someone suggests to us the existence of a document as important as the Coxe manuscript. We are prepared to take it off your hands."

"Take it off my hands?"

"Buy it from you. It's in your interest to sell it to us. We know how to dispose of it. You do not. We have the contacts. You do not."

"How do you know I don't?"

"Mr. Howard, not only do we know which academic institutions are willing, indeed anxious, for such an acquisition, we also know of prominent private collectors who would be interested. You're a secondhand dealer, Mr. Howard, selling twenty-five and fifty-cent books. Make things simple for yourself. Leave the trading in rare books and manuscripts to experts in the field, such as we at the Newberry Gallery."

"How much?" he asked.

"Fifteen hundred."

"Dollars?"

"Precisely."

"You're nuts, Miss Kelly. You know the manuscript is worth a hell of a lot more than that."

"Well, I won't quibble. We're prepared to offer you two thousand."

"The hell you will," he said. "I happen to know that the Coxe manuscript is worth up to eight or ten thousand dollars."

"You may believe so, Mr. Howard. But even if it is, what good is it to you if you don't have a buyer? Certainly you're not a private collector yourself, unless you're keeping your rarities a secret." She laughed. "And I seriously doubt that."

"Sorry, Miss Kelly. I'm not saying I have or don't have the manuscript. But even if I did, it ain't for sale."

"You're being foolish, Mr. Howard. Three thousand!"

"Three!" he rubbed his head and thought a minute. "Nix, not even at three."

Miss Kelly dropped the Gauloise to the floor and ground it out with the ball of her high-heeled shoe.

"There are other factors to consider, Mr. Howard. Vital ones. You do not have the expertise to determine the authenticity of the document. We are experts. In addition, there may be reason to suspect that the manuscript is stolen. If it is, and you attempt to sell it, the sale could be ruled invalid. You could lose not only the sale but the manuscript. Now, we are prepared to take the burden from you completely."

"Absolutely not, Miss Kelly. I've decided."

The maverick streak Howard inherited from his old man had come out. Once he made up his mind, Pop never changed it. Harry was like that, too. Harry once told Pop that of all known subjects, from aviation to xylophone playing, he had fixed and invariable ideas that had not altered since he was four years old.

"Four thousand dollars! Mr. Howard. Our final offer."

It was, of course, his way out. He could take the money; they would take the manuscript. He would pay back First National Bank and old man Butterman. He would buy back his Nash. Return to Canal Street and retrieve his furnishings. Everything would be just the way it was before. Before William Trevor Coxe, before Ronald Newberry, before Richard James Larch. There would be Howard and Brummell, and Jacob Bluestein across the street, and Ann Elkin spending her life writing a novel no one was going to publish. There would be the dust, the battered books, their pages falling out, the old magazines with their corners turning up. But there wouldn't be any Lenny.

"Miss Kelly, I'm not the smartest guy in the world. Didn't even get out of Evander Childs High School in the Bronx. There's a lot of things I don't know, specially about rare manuscripts. But I know this. If I don't do something now to make some changes in my life, I'm gonna wind up like my old man and my friends Jacob Bluestein and Wolfgang Gottesman."

"If you're not careful, Mr. Howard, you may also wind up like Lenny Gould."

"I'm on to you and Newberry, lady! I know how you cleaned out Mrs. Whitten's apartment on Riverside Drive."

"That, that was a legitimate purchase! Arranged by her heir."

"Yeah, and I bet a lot of questions could be asked about how she died. Poor old lady. Heart attack, my ass!"

"How dare you!"

"And don't think I don't know you're involved with this killer Larch."

"Absurd!"

She turned angrily and ran to the door but couldn't open it because it was locked.

"I'll get it for you, Roberta," he said.

"It's *Miss Kelly!*"

After she left, he put on his overcoat, tucked the Coxe manuscript under his arm, made sure the CLOSED sign was on the door, and locked up. Still alert for Larch, he changed subway trains four times to make sure he wasn't being followed to Thirty-first Street.

The morning's winter sun flooded the massive pillars of Pennsylvania Station with light. Millions of particles of dust were shimmering in the rays. Even though he was one of thousands of people hurrying antlike to and from the trains below, he was humbled by the station's main concourse. A palace. The ornate ceiling rose like a grand cathedral's. Despite the activity, the station seemed eerily quiet, its vastness absorbing the babel of thousands of tongues. Most of man's creations might disappear but there was one thing of which he was sure. Pennsylvania Station was built on too grand a scale to ever fall. Like Fourth Avenue, it would always be there. He took some comfort in believing that.

18

Fifteen twenty-four Hollins Street," he told the cabbie. "You know where that is?"

"Sure, Buddy. Everyone knows where *that* is."

The Checker pulled from Baltimore's Pennsylvania Station south onto St. Paul Street and moved into heavy traffic, dodging Nashes, Packards, and Studebakers. A few blocks later, they passed a regal square on their right commanded by a tall monument.

"That's Mount Vernon Square," the cabbie said. "Washington Monument. George is way up on top. It's been there a lot longer than that other monument in D.C."

The driver turned right at Fayette Street.

"That's the courthouse," he said, motioning with his thumb at a self-important stone edifice disappearing behind them.

The tall downtown buildings gave way to narrow brick row houses, two and three stories high, each with its private set of white marble steps. The driver made a left at Stricker Street and then a right onto Hollins.

"Neighborhood's not what it used to be. Was all white. If it wasn't so cold, you'd be seeing a lot of niggers in the doorways. Lotta changes in Baltimore and none of 'em good."

The driver hit the breaks.

"Union Square," he said, pointing to his left. It was a small park that occupied the block, its trees bare and shivering in the winter cold, a frozen pond flanked by a building intended to resemble a Greek temple. A block of row houses overlooked the park.

"This is it, buddy. Fifteen twenty-four Hollins. That'll be sixty-five cents."

Howard paid the driver, gave him a dime tip, and got out, clutching the Coxe manuscript under his arm. A gust of cold wind sucked at his breath. Harry's, like the others, was a narrow three-story red-brick building with a handrail leading up seven white marble steps. Nothing but the number to distinguish it from the rest. There were white shutters on the windows. He went up the steps and rang the bell at the arched doorway and waited for several minutes before he pressed the button again. Finally, the door opened a crack. A younger, thinner version of Harry peered out, wiping his hands on a towel.

"Sorry, I didn't hear you," he said. "I was in the kitchen."

"Ah, is Harry home? I'm an old friend. I've got to see him."

"Impossible. We are taking no visitors. We had to turn away Evelyn Waugh."

"I've come all the way from New York City."

"My brother sees no one."

"You're Harry's—?"

"I'm August."

Another gust of wind whipped up the steps.

"Please. May I come in for a moment? It's so cold."

"Well . . ." August took his coat.

In the living room, Howard stood in front of a feeble blaze in a fireplace protected by an ornate iron grill, watching his reflection in the large mirror over the mantel. To the left was a secretary filled with books and a curtain over a doorway that must have led to the dining room.

"I didn't know Harry was sick," Howard said.

"A stroke," August said, shaking his head. "He had had perhaps three strokes before but they were mild. On November 23rd, he had a massive one."

August sat on a footstool by a French chair.

"It was a hard summer for him, you know," he said, sounding weary. "The Baltimore *Sun* wanted him to cover the national conventions."

"Jeez, Harry sure didn't look like a newspaperman," Howard said.

"He's a reporter down to his boots, just part of everything else he's accomplished. You've heard of his coverage of the Scopes trial in Tennessee?"

"The what?"

"The Monkey Trial? Forget it. It was a long time ago. Anyway, he went to the Republican Convention in Philadelphia in June, but it was so hot that he felt ill and had to come home. He *is* sixty-eight, you know. But he was better in July and went back to Philadelphia to see Truman nominated by the Democrats. Then he went back again for the Progressive Convention. He seemed to be all right, his usual, crusty self, although he had been complaining about losing his memory. Even though he had been working steadily, he used to tell me that his mind started to deteriorate in 1945, that he would become nervous and confused whenever he sat down at the typewriter."

"What happened when he had his stroke?" Howard asked.

"It was just two weeks after the election. He was visiting his secretary, Mrs. Lohrfinck. He was holding a drink. Then he said he had a headache. He dropped the glass and began talking incoherently. Mrs. Lohrfinck called Dr. Baker, who rushed over. My brother began accusing Dr. Baker of being Stalin; he began ranting about Roosevelt. Dr. Baker and Mrs. Lohrfinck got him down the elevator and into the doctor's car and drove him to Johns Hopkins Hospital. We thought he was going to die! He had a cerebral thrombosis that paralyzed his entire right side and his speech center. *My brother can't speak anymore!*"

August began shaking and put his hands to his face. Then he was calm.

"Oh, maybe a word or two, unintelligibly," he said. "Just grunts mostly."

"Jeez."

"After three weeks in the hospital, he could walk around a little. With help. The doctors sent him home after five weeks."

"He's here? Harry's *here*?"

"He's in his study."

"Why can't I—"

"It would do no good. He can't communicate. We think he can hear and maybe understand at least a little of what is being told to him. But he just sits in his chair and stares. He can't read, can't write. Mrs. Lohrfinck has to answer his letters. I was afraid he might get up in the middle of the night and fall down the stairs, so I put a little gate at the top like they do for very small children."

"My pop died of a stroke," Howard said. "Pop was a little older than Harry but they were good friends."

"What did your father do?"

"He ran a bookstore in New York."

"Ah, yes. My brother reserved every third week to go to New York City. He edited magazines, you know. *Smart Set* and *The American Mercury*. He would also shop there for musical scores for his Saturday Night Music Club. But he swore he'd never leave Baltimore permanently. In fact, he was just three when our family purchased this house in 1883. He's lived here almost all of his life. Except for a short time when he was married and lived in an apartment on Cathedral Street."

"I never knew Harry was married."

"A short one, alas. Sara died after five years of marriage and my brother moved back to Hollins Street. I've lived here all my life. I'm nine years younger than my brother."

"Somehow, Harry didn't seem the type for marriage."

"My brother used to say to me that for him Elysium was the end of the day and the sight of a woman, mature but still beautiful, with a low-pitched voice, sitting at the edge of a divan talking to him, close enough for him to reach out and touch her hand. He would say that nothing could be more beautiful."

"I've known Harry off and on since I was a kid and never knew that side of him. He was a regular at my pop's store, you know."

"My brother had an affinity for book dealers. One of his closest friends is Siegfried Weisberger, who owns the Peabody Bookshop and Beer Stube on North Charles Street." August began chuckling. "My brother had a trick he used to play on poor Mr. Weisberger. He would pick up some odd volume on the table out front, take it in, and sell it for ten cents or a quarter. Weisberger never knew he was buying his own book."

"No!"

"I can tell you something else. My brother used to swipe Gideon Bibles by the dozen and at Christmastime send them to his friends inscribed, 'with the compliments of the author.' "

"Harry's not that kind of guy," Howard said.

"He had his own kind of humor." August stood up. Would you like some tea?" he offered.

"Sure. Thanks. But listen . . ." Howard put his hand on August's arm. "Can't I see Harry for just a minute?"

"Well . . ."

"Maybe he'll remember me. Maybe it would help."

"Really, it won't work. My brother is only a shell."

"Please."

August shook his head, then shrugged his shoulders. "If you insist." He took Howard up the stairs to Harry's study on the second floor. Harry was slouched in a heavy leather chair, staring vacantly, an old man whose parts had worn out. He was wearing a dark suit, the coat open to reveal red suspenders. He had on a white shirt and a wide tie with a floral pattern. August had dressed him as usual, as if for work.

"Hi, Harry," Howard said.

There was no answer.

The windows of the room overlooked Union Square across the street. There were no curtains or drapes. An old-fashioned typewriter sat silent on a table next to a huge desk. A pipe rack was on the desk with several long-extinguished corncob pipes. There was an ashtray on a stand but no sign of Harry's beloved Uncle Willies. An electric fan was in the corner, turned off for the winter. File cabinets stood against the wall. Everywhere there were carefully placed stacks of books, books that Harry couldn't read. Everything was neat. As though for a photographer.

"I'll brew the tea and bring you a cup," August said.

"Thanks."

As August left the room, Howard pulled over a chair and sat directly across from Harry.

"Well," he said, "I guess it'll be a while before you come back into my store, selling me my own books."

No answer, just a dull-eyed stare. What was left of that once great mind? Could it be that the real Harry was deep inside that head, as if within some dark cave, looking out?

"I went ahead and did it, Harry. I bought the manuscript I was telling you about. You know, the one by that Englishman who wrote a firsthand account of the French Revolution. I paid a lot of money for it, Harry. Everything I had and more. I need to find a buyer. You know about books and libraries and things. You gotta help me. I didn't even get out of Evander Childs High School. You told me that if I needed help, I could come to you and I did."

Harry's once-pudgy frame leaned in the chair, his mouth drooped a little, his hands were in his lap.

"Things have been bad, Harry. Someone's killed my brother and they're out to get me! That's right, Harry, *Lenny's dead*. They killed him! Nobody knows Lenny was my half-brother except Ann Elkin. And now you. And Pop, of course. But he's dead, too. Even Lenny didn't know. The manuscript is my only hope. If I sell it, I can start over someplace else. Miami Beach. Me and Ann Elkin."

A thin line of saliva ran down Harry's jaw.

"Look at it, Harry. Here's the manuscript." Howard took it out of its box and held it before his face. "See, it's authentic. You can tell. Look at those funny letters. Harry, I know you can't read it yourself, so I'm going to read some of it to you. I want you to hear it. It's an important document. 1790. Listen to this, Harry, 'I had been to Paris twice the previous fall and was quite familiar with its fortifications . . .' " He read haltingly because he wasn't all that good a reader.

Suddenly Harry's head moved slightly as if he was trying to raise it. His left hand jiggled, his little finger wiggled but just barely.

"What is it, Harry?"

No answer.

He read on. Harry seemed to be trying to move his head again; his finger rose maybe half an inch.

"You heard something, didn't you, Harry? Something's wrong. A *word*. It was a word, right?"

Harry's eyes remained clouded but the little finger of his left hand quivered again as if in agreement.

"But which word?"

He started reading again from the beginning.

Again a twitch. It seemed to come on the word *to* in the sentence. "I had been *to* Paris twice the previous fall . . ." A twitch came again when Howard got to the word *fall*. He read on. Harry made some more movements when Howard reached the words *stores* and *cafes* and *near-engagements*. Harry might have been agitated but it was hard to tell.

He put the manuscript down. "Harry, you're telling me something's not right."

August came into the room with a tray containing a cup of steaming tea.

"What *are* you doing?" he asked.

"I, I'm reading to Harry."

"Reading what?"

"An old manuscript called *An Englishman's Account of the Revolution of 1789 and the Taking of the Bastille*."

August put the tray down on a table. "We read to my brother all the time," he said, "but it does no good. He cannot understand."

"But I think he does. I think he's found something wrong with the manuscript, certain words. Flaws."

"And how is he doing that?"

"Well, his finger twitches."

August shook his head. "Means nothing. My brother twitches all the time. It's involuntary."

"But he seemed to signal at certain words."

"The stroke has caused enormous damage. Dr. Baker says that

in time, perhaps, he will get better, possibly be able to communicate in some way. But not now."

"May I read a little more?"

"I suppose so."

Howard began reading again. Every so often there would be another movement of Harry's left hand, a twitch of the finger.

"You know," Howard said. "I'd better write down those words. They must mean something. Please, may I have a pencil and paper?"

"You *can't* go on. Can't you see that my brother is getting tired."

"Just another paragraph. Please."

"Well . . ."

Howard read the entire page to Harry. On the pad August had given him, he scribbled down the words that Harry seemed to single out. By this time Harry's face had become flushed. Perspiration ran in rivulets from his hairline and down his cheeks. Droplets of sweat bubbled on the backs of his hands.

"Enough!" August said. "You must leave the room."

Howard sighed, put the manuscript back into its box, and snapped the rubber bands around it. Harry's jaw had grown slacker. He was depleted, exhausted, and soaking wet. Howard stood up.

"Sorry to see you this way, Harry," he said, brushing away the tears from his eyes. He stood there for a long time looking down at him. Harry stared unfocused at the floor. God, Harry, how you used to think. Walked and talked like the rest of us, Howard thought, and what a mind you had. You enraged men like my old man but you also made them stand back in awe.

"So long, Harry."

Downstairs, Howard sat in the French chair near the fireplace.

"I really don't understand what you were doing, sir, reading that document to my brother," August said.

"Harry told me once that if I ever needed help, I could come to him. So I did. I always thought he was some kind of expert on language."

"He was. *Is!* He wrote a major book on the American language. There's a copy on that table. In fact, a supplement to it came out just a few months ago. He used to say that that book would outlast anything else he ever wrote and that he would be remembered longest as a student of language. My brother once said that for a hundred years, it will be difficult for anyone to write about American speech without mentioning him."

"Harry really was . . . *is* a special guy."

"Special? Around here he's known as the Sage. In the 1920s Walter Lippmann said—"

"Who?"

"Lippmann, Lippmann! Don't you read the papers? He said my brother was the most powerful personal influence on a whole generation of educated people. My brother was described as an American Shaw. They used to say his friend and colleague George Jean Nathan was an American Wilde. Let me show you something!" August went through the curtain into the other room and returned carrying a framed poem.

"This verse by Berton Braley was in the New York *Sun* in 1920," he said. "As you can tell, my brother infuriated people. They hated his intellectual power and influence. Read it."

There were three that sailed away one night
  Far from the maddening throng;
And two of the three were always right
  And everyone else was wrong.
But they took another along, these two
  To bear them company,
For he was the only one who ever knew
  Why the other two should be;
And so they sailed away, these three
  Mencken
  Nathan
  And God.

And the two they talked of the aims of Art,
  Which they alone understood;
And they quite agreed from the start

That nothing was any good
Except some novels that Dreiser wrote
And some plays from Germany.
When God objected they rocked the boat
And dropped him into the sea,
"For you have no critical facultee,"
Said Mencken
And Nathan
To God.

The two came cheerfully sailing home
Over the surging tide.
And trod once more on their native loam
Wholly self-satisfied;
And the little group that calls them great
Welcomed them fawningly,
Though why the rest of us tolerate
This precious pair must be
Something nobody else can see
But Mencken
And Nathan
And God!

August began laughing. "My brother loved it!" he said. "He thought it was charmingly funny. But that was in the twenties. In the thirties, my brother lost a lot of his influence. It might have been because he hated Roosevelt so much, maybe because he was so inflexible. His ideas became, well, a little out-of-date."

"I hope Harry gets better," Howard said, putting his hand on August's shoulder.

"I'm taking him to Daytona in February and then to Gertrude's farm. She's our sister. All we can do is pray."

"Something Harry would never do."

19

He walked down the marble steps of 1524 Hollins Street and into the cold, the box with the manuscript under his arm. The biting wind whipped around him as he cut across Union Square to look for a cab on Lombard Street. He put the collar of his overcoat up and held his hat on his head with his hand. He hailed a Checker, intending to return to the station to catch the next train to New York, but then he changed his mind.

"Say, cabbie, do you know where the Peabody Bookshop and Beer Stube is on North Charles Street?"

"Course, mister. Everyone knows where *that* is."

North Charles was too narrow to be a noble thoroughfare but there was an elegance about many of the stores. Money was spent there. The taxi stopped in front of the bookstore, a little seedy, not quite in keeping with the neighborhood. But bigger and better kept than Howard's own place.

"Fifty cents, mister."

The usual tables of cheap books, held down by rocks to protect them from the snarling wind, were on either side of the doorway. He swept a book from one of the tables as he went in. Familiar sagging shelves of books commanded the front of the store. A more narrow book-lined passageway led to the rear, from which he could hear the sound of music. A zither. A sharp-nosed man sat behind the cash register, reading.

"Pardon me," he said.

"Yeah?"

"Wonder if you might be interested in buying this book?"

"What is it?" He ripped it out of Howard's hands and opened it. "*The House of the Seven Gables*. Think I gotta couple copies of that. What the hell! Give you a dime for it."

"Sold."

He reached into his pocket and flipped Howard a dime. He had a slight European accent. German, maybe.

"What's the music I hear?"

"That's a zither. Girl comes in to play most every evening. Sometimes there's a juggler. A magician. Serve drinks and food in the back."

"That's unusual for a bookstore, isn't it? Drinks?"

"It's survival, my friend. People don't have to read but they want to eat and drink. The Age of the Boob is upon us."

"You're a cheerful sort."

"What's to be cheerful? I predict very dark days for America. The people, they don't want books and ideas and culture. They only want dollars. I'm planning to sell out in a couple of years and move to the Eastern Shore. Then the Peabody Bookshop will fade away just like the others. I mean, what's this new thing coming in? Television. What do you think *that's* going to do to reading? Who's going to pick up a book when some pabulum is spewed at them on a screen night and day? Where's the incentive? Now, excuse me, mister, there are other things I gotta do. Like read this book."

In exaggerated style, he returned to whatever it was he was reading. Howard chuckled. The proprietor could have been a product of Fourth Avenue. Howard browsed a bit, not interested in anything except the M's. He found several books written by Harry and pulled one off the shelf because it looked like the cheapest since it had no dust jacket and was battered in a friendly manner. He went back to the cash register.

"Ahem."

"Yeah?"

"I'd like to buy this," he said.

The dealer opened it. "Ah, *Happy Days*." He seemed to relax. "That's one of his best books. 1940. You read it before?"

"No."

"Didn't think so or you wouldn't be buying it. About his grow-ing-up days here in Baltimore. It's a recollection of his childhood. Precocious kid, he was. The book's warm. Some people wouldn't describe him that way. But I would. You'll like it. *If* you're a reader." He looked at Howard with justified skepticism.

"How much?"

"For you, a dollar and a quarter."

Howard took his wallet out of his back pocket. "You knew him, didn't you?" he said.

"Knew him? I *know* him. You talk like he's dead!"

"Well, I know he's had this stroke—"

"Listen, mister, he's gonna survive it. You can't destroy a man like that. You know, one day before I met him, I saw one of his books remaindered on a sales table at a drugstore. A goddamned drugstore! So I bought it. I mean a drugstore, with its displays of Sal Hepatica and Quinsana Foot Powder and Vitalis! So I wrote him and I said that a *bookstore* like *mine* would be more proper for his books than some damn place that sells toilet articles. He wrote me back. We became friends. I began to put together a col-lection of his books and manuscripts, which wasn't easy because he saved everything, even his family recipes! You know, he liked my idea of serving beer in the back of the store. He wrote me once that I had the right formula, that when things got too unpleasant for him, he'd burn the day's newspaper, pull down the curtains, get out the jugs, and put in a civilized evening. He liked the sauce all right."

"You're the owner of this store?"

"Weisberger. Siegfried Weisberger."

Howard opened his wallet, pulled out a dollar bill, and handed it to him. From his side pocket, he removed a quarter and gave that to him, too. Weisberger hit the cash register key and flipped the money inside. He had his dime back and more.

"Yeah, he liked the stuff okay. I'll never forget the night of April 6, 1933. The Great Evening. The end of Prohibition. The end of the Horror, as he called it. His friends Paul Patterson and Hamilton Owens and Harry Black joined him at the round bar at the Rennert Hotel. They got there just before midnight. My friend was surrounded by the curious, the thirsty, the photographers. He took the first legally dispensed stein and said, 'Here it goes!' He downed it and smiled. 'Not bad!' he said. Civilization had returned to Baltimore, by God! He used to say that alcohol is an absolute necessity. Even automobiles need it."

Howard laughed at that.

Weisberger scratched his armpit. "You know, he could never understand the man who had violent likes and dislikes in his choice of booze. The guy who adores highballs but despises malt liquor or who dotes on white wine but hates red or insists that Scotch whiskey prolongs life, while rye causes cancer. He used to say he saw merit in every alcoholic beverage ever created by man and drank 'em all."

Weisberger crammed *Happy Days* into a paper bag and thrust it at Howard.

"I'll never forget that Saturday Night Club of his," Weisberger said. "Use to sit in on it all the time. There was Max Broedel and Thedor Hemberger and Fred Gottlieb and Louis Cheslock. What music they made! And what fights they had over what they would play."

"Harry played an instrument?"

"Piano! He played waltzes, polkas, schottisches, mazurkas. But he preferred the German composers."

"I knew he had strong ideas about music but I never knew Harry was a musician himself."

"Mister, let me tell you something. The Saturday Night Club was famous. Famous! Then, how would you know? Its heyday was in the twenties when it met at Al Hildebrand's violin shop on Fayette Street. Then they moved it to the Rennert Hotel and later to Schellhase's Restaurant on Howard Street. During the good years my friend would always be the first to arrive. Promptly at eight. Precisely at ten, they adjourned to the nearest watering hole. They played Beethoven, Brahms, Mozart, Haydn. At one time, the club was a dozen strong. A year or so ago, there were barely enough members to form a trio, and some of them were so old they could hardly lift their instruments. Harry would say half of the members were senile, the other half insane. Now that he's incapacitated, the days of the Saturday Night Club are few, just like secondhand book stores. You mark my words!"

Weisberger's eyes began to sparkle. He pulled out a handkerchief from his back pocket, wiped the tears from his eyes, and blew his nose.

"Step in the back," he said. "I wanna buy you a stein."

"No, I—"

"It's on the house."

The girl playing the zither strummed a lovely ballad. The tune was familiar but Howard couldn't recall its name. It had a haunting quality to it. Like "Nature Boy."

The lights of the little towns of Maryland, Delaware, and New Jersey flashed on the other side of the windows of the coach as it chugged north to New York. He put his head back on the seatrest. The locomotive was burning coal and he could see a haze of dust dimly reflected in the nearly empty railroad car. He started to sneeze and pulled a handkerchief from his pocket. Harry used to tell Pop that the cost of a parlor-car seat was the best investment in America because in a Pullman, the people were clean and did not smell badly. Harry would bitch about the day-coach stinks, babble, noise. And the imbecile conversation of the hoi polloi, as he would say. Well Harry, Howard thought, it would still have to be coach for him until William Trevor Coxe came through.

In spite of freezing temperatures outside the Pennsylvania Railroad car, he began to sweat, thinking about what Harry may have been trying to tell him in the privacy of that lonely study. He pulled out the piece of paper on which he had written the words Harry appeared to have flagged, and read them again. "To," "fall," "stores," "cafes," "near-engagements."

Aw, Harry, what did they mean? Nothing, of course, the meaningless words of a once-great man, now torn to rubble. Harry.

And Howard needed him so much.

20

"I'm telling you I'm getting a goddamned raw deal and you're gonna to do something about it!"

Nearly three hundred pounds of flesh were crushing him. Howard could scarcely breathe. Larch had caught up to him again.

It happened almost as soon as Howard had returned to 80½. He thought he had been careful, making sure he hadn't been followed. He locked the door behind him as soon as he walked in and pulled the long string to turn on the bare light bulb that dangled from the ceiling. A hungry Brummell the cat pelted him with a paw. He put the box with the Coxe manuscript on top of a stack of *National Geographics*, grabbed a container of cat food, and knelt down to sprinkle some dried pellets into Brummell's bowl. Suddenly, there was a shattering of glass and a splintering sound as a mass of protein crashed into the room and collapsed on top of him!

Brummell jumped sideways into the air with terror in his cat eyes and vanished. Howard's face was pushed into the cat's bowl and the dried cat food crumbled against his lips, tasting mealy. No wonder Brummell was always so angry.

"You've been keeping out of sight, bookseller, but I knew you'd turn up sooner or later! Now, I've got you."

"You're going to kill me," Howard managed to say, flakes of cat food falling from his lips.

The pressure eased from his back as Larch sat up. Then he felt something cold and steel-like against the flesh behind his ear.

"I'm climbing off of you, bookseller, but if you move, I'll blow your head off."

Howard began to breathe again as the weight was lifted from him. A meaty hand grabbed his collar and as Larch rose, Howard was pulled to a standing position.

"Stay where you are," Larch said. He backed to the splintered door. A gun tiny and silver looked like a toy in his huge hand. It was aimed at Howard's chest. He closed what was left of the frame, making sure the shade was pulled as far down as it could go. The wind outside fluttered the shade, forcing a cold current around it through the broken glass into the already chilled room.

"All right, where is it?"

"Where's what?"

He moved forward quickly and pushed the barrel of the pistol into Howard's mouth.

"You really do want a hole in the back of your neck, don't you, wise guy? Let's have some answers."

"The manuscript?" Howard managed to say after his mouth was cleared, the bitter metal an aftertaste.

"The *Coxe* manuscript."

"My ticket to Miami Beach. Christ, Larch, why are you so anxious to kill over a manuscript? There must be cleaner ways of making money."

"It's not the money, bookseller. Sit down. I want to talk to you."

"But—"

"On the floor. Sit down!"

Howard lowered himself to the dusty floor, the boards creaking under the weight of his behind, wishing he had used the broom a little more often. Larch loomed over him like a brontosaurus.

"Okay," he said, "so I'm not honest. I'm a crook. But I've never killed for money."

"Baloney. Lenny—"

"That's different! Look, the FBI wants me from here to California. I stand a good chance of doing a lot of time, if I'm caught. And I may not be able to hide forever. But it's one thing to do time for theft and it's another to burn for murder. They keep the hot seat warmed up at Sing Sing, you know. And I don't intend to fry. That's why I need that manuscript you've got and that's why I need it now. It's proof they're giving me a bum rap. Besides, if it's worth money to you, it's worth money to me. I'd make a lot more green from it than you'd ever get."

Larch sank onto a pile of books. He balanced his right arm on his knee, the gun pointing between Howard's eyes.

"Who are you, Larch? You don't seem like a usual thief. Books. Manuscripts. How many crooks know anything about those?"

"What do you want, bookseller, my resume?"

"I was just asking—"

"Stocks and bonds." Droplets of sweat began running down his face, despite the chill.

"Huh?"

"Stocks and bonds. That's how I started. Out on the Coast. I went to UCLA. Business degree. Worked for Landau, Coffman, Neavill, and Cruikshank, third-biggest brokerage firm in the country. I got to know my clients, their interests, hobbies, the things they needed, the things they *wanted*. These were well-heeled guys. When one client of mine said he needed a certain rare numismatic book, I went to the UCLA library to find out about it. I thought maybe I could locate a copy for him somewhere. I did. Right in the UCLA library! I gave it to my client with my compliments. Oh, he insisted on paying me something for it, not what the book was worth, of course, but he was so damned grateful, he kept on buying more stocks and bonds from me. So I got him more numismatic books from the UCLA library. He paid me for them."

"So that's how it started," Howard said.

"Pretty soon, I was pegged as a guy who not only knew something about books but who could get hold of certain rare editions because of a little private dealership I ran on the side. One of my clients was a doctor who collected antique medical texts and said he would pay anything for the first surgical manual in English, Brunschwig's *Surgery,* printed in London by Petrus Trereris in 1525. That was a tough nut to crack but on a vacation east, I ran down a copy at Yale. To the people in New Haven, I was merely a doctor doing research. When I left, Yale was minus its *Surgery* and my client had a copy, for which he paid a pretty penny. Needless to say, I discovered I was on to something."

"But doesn't it take a lot of knowledge about old books?" Howard asked. "You had a background in stocks and bonds."

"I had to do my homework. I learned about bibliographies and catalogs and *American Book-Prices Current*. Discovered points, editions, states. As I began to acquire an inventory, I started to advertise in *Bookman's Weekly*. I was almost like a legitimate dealer except my only investment was time. And since I stashed the books in a spare bedroom, I had no overhead."

"You had to be afraid of getting caught."

"Getting caught? Never entered my mind. Most books lie dormant on library shelves for months or years. Then, if a copy here and there was discovered missing, it was usually chalked up to merely being misplaced. How could they trace the theft to me after all that time? And say I *did* get caught. We're talking about *books*, not real loot, not like money or jewelry or cameras. It would all be a mistake. I'd tell the cops it had just been an oversight. Chances would be I'd get off with just a fine. *If* they ever caught me."

"But the books you stole," Howard said. "Most of them were from libraries. You can always tell a library book."

"Yeah, most libraries screw up their books with shelf marks, perforations, stamps, bookplates, and card pockets. But I learned how to get rid of them. Not hard to do. I would carefully remove the marred page with a razor blade and tip in a new page cut from another book of about the same age and paper quality. The average collector wouldn't know anyway. Of course, the libraries don't maim the really good stuff. I got to know which libraries specialized in which books, how to pass myself off as a scholar."

"But something happened. You were found out."

"Something happened all right. No, nobody caught me stealing a book. Not yet. It happened when I decided to branch out into a little stock and bond business of my own, specializing in over-the-counter issues that were hard to trace. I became a kind of an independent discount broker, selling securities at cut-rate to some of my more-aware clients. I don't know how Landau, Coffman, Neavill, and Cruikshank caught on, but one evening when the FBI came knocking at my front door, I scrammed out the back. I decided it would be a lot safer somewhere else, so I hopped a Pullman to St. Louis. I lost a lot of inventory in that move but I was able to clean out my bank accounts before the G-men got wind of them. That ended my career as a broker."

"But apparently not as an independent book dealer," Howard said.

"Right," Larch said. "I quickly began to build an inventory again. College libraries were the best targets. They never had much security, if any. Bryn Mawr, Bucknell, DePauw, Georgetown, Missouri, Northwestern, Ohio Wesleyan, Oberlin, Denison, Antioch. Hell, most of them *still* don't know what they're missing. I kept good records. Stashed my inventory in various storage rooms. Used post office box numbers. Oh yes, obviously, I couldn't use my own name, so I adopted pseudonyms to contact my old clients and dealers. I had want lists from more than one dealer who weren't especially concerned about where the merchandise came from. At least, they never asked questions. It was business as usual."

With his left hand, Larch wiped at the perspiration on his forehead.

"But you got caught again."

"I had a run of bad luck. Happened at Wittenberg College in Ohio. I'm not the most inconspicuous guy around at six-foot-four. It was in the stacks. I had stashed a couple of books under my suit coat and I got careless. One of the books slid to the floor and some librarian saw it. She called a couple of campus security guards, big bruisers like myself, who held me long enough for the cops to get there. The cops hauled me to the local lockup, where they searched me and found a matchbook from the Hideaway Hotel, where I had been staying. Well, they got a search warrant, went to my room, and found about a hundred books owned by Wittenberg and several other colleges in the area, as well. They also found some false identification papers, my counterfeiting tools, and a loaded gun. They charged me with possession of stolen property and grand theft and held me on one-thousand-dollars bail."

"They let you go."

"Well, I called this woman I lived with in St. Louis, Betty, and she came up and bailed me out and we took off. I can tell you, there was no way I was going to go back and stand trial. Shit, I'd be in the cooler for five years. When I didn't show up for the court hearing, the FBI got into the act, found out I was wanted for interstate transportation of stolen stocks and bonds, and they issued a new federal warrant for my arrest. But this time, my lady friend and I were safe in Philadelphia, using new names and a new post office box. And I still had most of my inventory."

"You got careless again," Howard said.

"Shit, it wasn't my fault. It was a goddamned accident! Everything was going all right. I was working the library at Haverford College. I looked just like I said I was, a legitimate scholar, and I had letters of reference to prove it. Forged, of course. But how would they know? Then some smartassed librarian, some old coot with white hair and thick glasses, recognized me from my picture in a library journal. How was I to know the cops were going to release my mug shot? And to a bunch of librarians! The old codger brought in a campus cop and they tried to grab me. But I knew I couldn't be caught this time, so I let 'em have it. Punched the security guard in the stomach, slugged the old guy in the face, and ran out the back. I stumbled over a library cart and fell on my ass on the way out. Got a hell of a black eye. But made it to my car and escaped through the back roads before the cops arrived."

"It wasn't exactly a clean getaway, was it?" Howard said.

"I first thought I got away clean. But when I drove back to my hotel room that night, I saw that the cops had staked it out, so I just kept on going. Shit, the jerks had parked right outside in a police car. Then I realized my wallet was gone. It must have fallen out of my pocket when I tripped over the cart. I hadn't even known it. Normally, the cops couldn't have traced me through my wallet, since all the documents I carried were forged. But there was a receipt inside from the hotel I had been staying in. Christ, this time they *really* cleaned me out because I not only had a lot of inventory stashed in that room but my card file was in there, too. It cataloged my holdings. A lot of my books were stored in lockers. Now the cops knew what I had and where I had it stored. I was in trouble. Back to square one."

He scratched the side of his face with the barrel of the pistol, then pointed it at Howard again. Strands of Larch's silver hair were plastered to his forehead by sweat.

"So you had to start building up an inventory again fast," Howard said.

"Fast. That's why I came to New York. Wanted to work Columbia, the Morgan, the Frick, and the Bottom Collection. And to cash in some chips an associate of mine owed me."

"Now there's a murder charge against you."

"That's why you're going to give me that manuscript."

"I can't give it up."

"I tried to talk to you. I wanted to be reasonable. You really don't have a choice."

"Nix."

"It's your last chance."

"You're going to kill me?"

"Who said I was going to kill you?"

He stood up. He paced the floor for a bit. Then he came back to where Howard was squatting. Suddenly, there was a flash of silver in the dim light. Howard heard a thud and felt himself flying to his side against a pile of books. At first he felt no pain. Then the hurt began like cracks reaching out in a pane of glass and he realized that the noise he had heard was the sound of Larch's gun butt against his skull. He used his hand to try to pull himself up but his arm slipped and his head hit the floor. As the pain spread, he felt a wetness against his face and knew it was his own blood.

"That's only a taste," Howard heard Larch's voice say. "Here's another."

There was a blow to his stomach like the wind taking his breath away. Like the first blow, there was no sting at first, then a gradual agonizing pain in his rib cage. Larch had kicked him with a size-fifteen oxford.

"Want something else, book dealer?"

This time his hand grabbed Howard's neck, a compact fit behind fat fingers, which began to squeeze. He was crushing Howard's windpipe. Whether he meant to or not, Larch was killing him. Howard wanted to surrender. He tried to raise his hand to point at the manuscript, which wasn't hidden at all but was in its box on top of a stack of *National Geographics*, but he didn't have the strength. This time he was going. *Really* going. Like Lenny. Larch would leave him dangling from the ceiling and Klein the landlord would find him the next day twisting and turning, buoyant in the winter air that flowed through the broken door.

The denizens of Fourth Avenue would gather outside in shocked clusters and talk in hushed tones, their conversation ending abruptly as the police wheeled out a corpse under a white sheet and rolled it to a waiting hearse. "That's Howard under that sheet," Tannen would whisper. "He was like a cousin to me," Gottesman would say. "Who done this rotten thing?" Mandelbatt would demand. "I always knew Eighty and a half was jinxed," said Goldwater. And the hearse would head slowly up Fourth Avenue to Union Square and then right at Fourteenth street to the morgue. There would be no rush and no siren because there wasn't any emergency.

"Fucking Hun!" screamed a voice. Even in Howard's fading state, the voice was familiar. There was the sound of a thump, object to flesh. The pressure from his windpipe ended abruptly. He began to breath again in gasping chunks. "I know your kind. You're the kind that made me lose my leg!" shouted the voice.

Painfully, Howard rolled onto his back and looked up at the great shape of Larch, his eyes glassy.

"And here's another!"

Howard saw a battered wooden crutch arc through the air and connect against the side of Larch's head. Stunned, Larch dropped the gun, his tongue protruding. He seemed about to topple but somehow maintained his balance until the crutch smashed against his head again and he fell like a redwood to the floor, the impact raising clouds of dust.

"Jacob," Howard whispered through his scarred throat. "You saved my life."

Jacob Bluestein hopped on his one leg, trying to keep his balance, then brought his crutch to the floor to steady himself.

"Door was open, sonny, what was left of it. So I came right on in."

Howard smiled even though blood was streaming down his face.

"I can't get down to help you, sonny, or I might never get back up," he said. He held his arthritic hand out to Howard and helped him to his feet. "I was gonna watch *Studio One* on my Crosley tonight and have a couple of beers and jump between the sheets. And then I decided, no, I'm gonna see if Howard's in the store, 'cause I know that's where you've been sleeping lately, and make one more goddamned attempt to find out what's really going on. Now I think maybe I know. Who is that big ape, anyway?" Jacob motioned with his crutch.

Larch lay on his back like a whale dead on the sand. He was out cold, mouth open, short breaths heaving his gut.

"He's the killer, Jacob! He's the guy who murdered Lenny and now you got him. We gotta phone the police."

"I got him? *I* got the killer. You mean, I'm a hero?"

Bluestein let Larch have it one more time with the crutch, just like he said he would do.

21

Ann and Howard got off the number 1 train at 116th Street and walked across the big ugly campus that separated Low Memorial Library to the north from Butler Library to the south. The winter sun was almost warm and there were students lounging on the wide tiers of steps leading to the entrance of Low Memorial Library.

"I'm glad you're going to do this, Howard," Ann said.

"Well, Harry couldn't help me very much, poor bastard. But I know he was trying to tell me *something* about the manuscript." He carried the box with Mr. Coxe's scribblings under his arm. There was a bandage around his head, covering the wound Larch had given him. His rib cage still ached from Larch's kick. A secretary with tight black hair and tight lips showed them into Professor Svalgard's office in the history department in Fairweather Hall.

"Professor, I'm Ann Elkin. This is my friend, Howard—"

"Ah, Miss Elkin," the professor said, taking her hand. "Our mutual friend Edgar Ardery has told me about you and your interest in history. Let's see, Greece, Italy, ah, California. Perhaps I can interest you in France."

"I have an open mind."

He was tall and thin and wrinkled and wore a vested suit that displayed a gold watch chain with a Phi Beta Kappa key. A graying beard shaped like a billy goat's drooped from his chin.

"Please sit down, Miss Elkin. You, too, Mr. Howard."

"No, Howard's my f—"

"Now, Miss Elkin, I understand you have a rare document you wish me to examine."

"My friend does. Howard?"

He put the box on Svalgard's desk, took the rubber bands from around it, gingerly removed the manuscript, and placed it before him. The professor put on wire-rim spectacles and carefully lined the document up so that it faced him evenly. He cleared his throat as though he was going to read the manuscript to a class or a congregation. Then he opened it to the first page and started to read. Silently. Howard watched nervously as he did.

"Hmmmmm," Svalgard said suddenly, nodding his head. That seemed to be a sound of approval. He carefully turned a page, then another. "Very interesting," he said. He took off his glasses and held a page very close to his eyes. "Yes, yes," nodding his head again. He put his glasses back on and went to another page. Howard stood up and began pacing the small office that was lined with books, many in French, most very old. A globe of the planet lay in a wooden cradle. He gave the globe a spin and watched the continents and oceans merge. It was like waiting for a doctor to decide whether you had cancer.

> Harry had a low opinion of historians. He used to tell Pop that it was humanity's misfortune that its history was written mostly by third-rate men. Dunderheads, Harry called them.
>
> "Harry," Pop said, "if we don't have no history books, then we won't ever understand ourselves."
>
> "A good grammar text is more vital for you, my good bookseller," Harry said, firing an Uncle Willie. "It will never be possible to arrive at the precise truth about the majority of important historical events. At best, perhaps, we might learn half of what actually happened. The fact is, the historians have no desire to make the truth known about the half of history of which we are ignorant."
>
> "Why, Harry? Dammit, why would historians want to hide fifty percent of the truth. Makes no sense."
>
> "Because those of that ilk rarely rise above the level of pedagogues on the one hand, while the others are nothing more than highly prejudiced partisans."

Svalgard cleared his throat, bringing Howard back to Morningside Heights. "Ah, Mr. Howard," he said. "I think you have something here." The professor sat still for a moment and seemed to stare into space. "I wonder if I might take possession of the manuscript for a while."

Howard ran over to the desk and protectively put his hand on the document.

"I meant for further study, Mr. Howard, not to keep."

"No!" Howard said. "No one takes this baby."

Svalgard took off his glasses and put them on the desk. "I can understand your reluctance, of course, but I believe you have made a real historical find and it deserves a more-detailed look."

"Then it's authentic?"

"As far as I can tell without additional examination."

"Then there *was* a William Trevor Coxe, just like Lenny said?"

"There was a William Trevor Coxe, *indeed*. A very shadowy figure of the eighteenth century who, as a foreigner, appeared to to have played an important but secret role in what the loyalists thought were efforts to save the monarchy of Louis the Sixteenth. *However*, there arc rumors that he tried to engineer an armed intervention by George the Third and came very close. In fact, there are hints that Coxe may have had a secret relationship with the Marquis de Mirabeau, one of the greatest intellects of the early Revolution. Mirabeau was despised by his own class because he supported the aims of the revolutionary movement. At the same time, he was hated by the masses because he seemed to favor a benign monarchy. Mirabeau died in 1791, so it's impossible to say how he may have altered the course of the Revolution and to what degree, if any, he was influenced by the machinations of William Trevor Coxe. Your manuscript may give us vital clues."

Svalgard rose from his seat and went to the window to look out over Amsterdam Avenue. "Revolution in France was inevitable. As early as 1762, Rousseau predicted what he called a time of crisis and a century of revolution. Now, what would happen were England to take advantage of the armed chaos that divided its historic enemy and stage an invasion? A very *careful* invasion plotted by William Trevor Coxe. This manuscript may well shed light on how much England was behind the French Revolution and what it hoped to gain from it."

"Wow, so Lenny was right!" Howard almost kissed the old goat.

Svalgard pulled at his whiskers. "For the scholar, the years 1789 to 1794 are rich in political, social, and cultural history. Thousands of decrees and laws covering every facet of existence were handed down by that poor, hapless Louis the Sixteenth and the revolutionary administrations that followed. A period of turmoil and terror. There's a wealth of bibliographic material of major revolutionary significance to be sure. But also such quixotic ephemera as the design of the deadly invention by Dr. Joseph-Ignace Guillotin and an account of the last days of Louis the Sixteenth and his family by the monarch's valet, Baptiste-Antoine Clery."

Howard stood up and grabbed Ann's hand. "Let's go, Ann, we

got some celebrating to do!" Then he stopped. "But, Harry, he *also* knew something about the manuscript. He just couldn't tell me. What could it have been?" A feeling of gloom wiped away the sense of celebration.

Svalgard turned from the window. "Mr. Howard, I don't know who this Harry is, but I implore you to leave the manuscript with me. To be absolutely certain of its authenticity we should have the paper analyzed. We have a laboratory here that will—"

"No lab's getting its hands on my manuscript!" Howard insisted.

"Howard—" Ann Elkin put her hand on his arm.

"Let me see the document again," the professor said. He sat down at the desk, put his glasses back on, and turned the pages. "Mr. Howard, there's a blank leaf at the very end. Nothing is written on it. Let me borrow that *one* leaf. That will have absolutely no impact on the value or historic worth of the manuscript. I have a colleague who is an expert on paper. He'll look at it. In a day or two, I will return the page to you. And that way, we'll know for sure."

"Well . . ."

"Do it, Howard," Ann coaxed.

Howard guessed Harry would have said to do it, too, so he did.

He and Ann walked across the campus toward Broadway. Howard carried the manuscript under his arm.

"It was the right thing to do, Howard, leaving that page with Professor Svalgard," she said.

He nodded.

"Things are all right now, aren't they, Howard? Lenny's killer is in jail. You've got your manuscript. And Edgar is giving me all sorts of *penetrating* advice about revising my novel."

"Yeah, Ann, Edgar's sticking it to you, all right."

Still, he couldn't get out of his mind the image of Harry, sprawled in his chair on Hollins Street, the all-but-useless finger moving just slightly with a warning.

"We humans are an inferior breed," Harry used to say to Pop, "and we probably deserve to be liquidated all together."

22

Mulvey dragged at a Lucky. Howard sat at the counter of 80½ pricing a stack of books a wino had brought in for sale in a cardboard carton. A carpenter that Klein the landlord had sent over had taken the plywood off the broken front door and was installing a new pane of glass.

"So what brings you to Fourth Avenue, Sergeant Mulvey?" Howard asked. "I thought the case was closed."

"Looks that way," Mulvey said. "Yeah, looks that way."

He started browsing through the shelves.

"Say, you got any good detective stuff?" he asked.

"Mysteries are in that section over there." Howard pointed.

Mulvey started poking through the books.

"Hey, how about this one?" He held up a book. "By S. S. Van Dine. Some Philo Vance story. Any good?"

"I don't read 'em, Sergeant, I only sell them."

He looked over the books a while longer, chose some, then came back to the front and dumped the books on the counter.

"I'll take these. See if I can learn something from them."

He had picked out books by Rex Stout, Ellery Queen, and John Dickson Carr. Howard opened each to the front flyleaf, where he had written the price, and then mentally added up the cost.

"That's two dollars. For you, a dollar seventy-five," he said.

Mulvey took a wallet out of his suit pocket and removed two bills.

"You want a bag?" Howard asked, flipping the cop his change.

"Ah, yeah. A bag. Might not be a good idea for the guys at the Twenty-third to see me walking in with an Ellery Queen."

"Come again, Sergeant."

The front door opened and shut several times. It was the carpenter testing his work. Mulvey still stood there holding his books, not making any move to leave, the Lucky dangling from the side of his mouth.

"Something wrong, Sergeant?"

"Frankly, Mr. Howard, I'm puzzled about a couple of things." He took the cigarette out of his mouth, threw it to the floor, and squashed it under his heel. Then he tossed his package of books back onto the counter. "Now, I've had a number of conversations with this guy Larch. It looks like we've got a pretty good case of murder against him. He's down at the Tombs waiting for trial. Then the Feds will have their turn at him."

He began to pace.

"This is what we have so far. First, Larch is a known criminal, although how much about his past crimes the judge will let the DA use against him in court we don't know yet. Second, there's plenty of evidence that Larch was in Lenny Gould's apartment the night of the murder. We have your testimony to that effect and that of Mrs. Jacobson, the landlady. It would be nothing for a powerful man like Larch to hang a skinny kid like Lenny Gould.

"As for a motive, we know that Larch was a notorious book and manuscript thief. Lenny Gould was also involved in the rare-book industry. He worked for you and he occasionally worked at the Caesar Auction Galleries on Madison Avenue. Both you and Ronald Newberry have stated that Lenny Gould had an interest in original manuscripts. We found four thousand dollars hidden in a sock in Lenny Gould's room, probably money either from the sale of or for the purchase of a rare book or manuscript. This leads us to conclude that Larch knew of the money, went to Lenny's apartment to rob him, but killed him instead. You interrupted Larch as he was searching for the money and he escaped." Mulvey took out another cigarette and lighted it. "Yeah, I think a jury will buy that. Only—"

"Only what?" Howard asked.

Mulvey blew a long stream of smoke through o-shaped lips. "Only he says he didn't do it."

"Christ, Mulvey, all criminals say that."

"Yeah." Mulvey nodded. "But Larch says he wasn't after the money. He was after a manuscript that he knew Lenny had. He says that when he got to the victim's room, Lenny was already dead."

"Already dead?" That's impossible, I—"

"You what?" Mr. Howard."

"Well, I—"

"Were you in Lenny's room earlier in the evening?"

"I, I . . ."

"We did a little more checking after interrogating Larch. You remember those old characters who play checkers out front of Lenny's house?"

Howard nodded.

"They told us they saw a guy that looks like you ring Lenny Gould's bell all right, just like you said you did. However, they recall that it was still light, dusk, when you went in. That would have made it around, say, seven-thirty, eight. Now, you tell us that you were attacked by Larch in Lenny's room a little after eleven. Mrs. Jacobson substantiates that. And, of course, that's when the precinct boys got the emergency call. Now, either you were in Lenny's apartment for some three hours or more or you were there twice, first in the early evening, the second in the late evening. How do you account for that, Mr. Howard?"

Howard shrugged in defeat and climbed off his stool. Now, with Larch behind bars, hiding the truth didn't seem to be as important.

"It's true, Sergeant, I was at Lenny's earlier in the evening. Then I went to P. J. Murphy's on the corner for a couple of drinks and I stayed to watch the Dodgers-Giants game on television. It was a no-hitter. Rex Barney. Then I realized I left a bottle of Scotch at Lenny's and went back to get it and that's when I ran into Larch."

Mulvey cocked his hat back onto his head.

"That's the truth," Howard said.

"What was the purpose of your initial visit to Mr. Gould?"

"I already told you. We saw each other all the time. I didn't have to have a purpose."

"Yeah, you were like *brothers*. You know, Mr. Howard, talking to you, I feel like a dentist pulling teeth. Now you said before that you went to see Lenny Gould in order to pick up some books he had borrowed from your store. Did you do that?"

"Well—"

"Did you leave Lenny Gould's room with those books? Did you leave Lenny Gould's with anything?"

Howard spread his hands helplessly.

"*Anything?*"

Howard plopped back down onto his stool. "I'm gonna admit something to you, Sergeant. Lenny and I had a deal going and I was afraid that if you found out about it, well, it might fall through."

"A deal involving some manuscript."

"Yeah."

"That Larch wanted."

"I guess so."

"So why didn't you tell me that earlier? It would have helped in our investigation. You know what you can get for withholding evidence?"

"What?"

"I dunno. But we're gonna find out."

"Sergeant, what's the gripe? You got your man. It doesn't matter whether he was after money or a manuscript. He's the killer!"

Mulvey pulled out a toothpick from the inside breast pocket of his suit coat and stuck it between his teeth. "How do you suppose Larch found out about the manuscript in the first place?"

"Well, it was his business. He had clients and dealers on his mailing list for years. He knew what titles they were after and he knew where to get them. The antiquarian-book business isn't that big. There aren't many secrets knocking around. Look, Sergeant, the guy was a thief. He packed a gun. He's been known to use it. Sooner or later, he was bound to murder someone. It turned out to be Lenny. And I got something else for you. Larch may have murdered someone else."

Mulvey's toothpick fluttered up and down between his teeth.

"There was this old lady on Riverside Drive and 100th," Howard said. Name of Whitten. Mrs. Gertrude Whitten. Had a lot of valuable books."

"So?"

"She's dead."

"You think Larch murdered her."

"Well, the doorman said she died of natural causes. But I'm sure Larch did it. Check it out."

"You have some reason to think Larch killed her?"

"Look, Sergeant, I had a run-in with Larch outside the old lady's apartment house. He must have been hanging around up there."

Mulvey retired his toothpick and took another Lucky out of his shirt pocket and lit it. "Terrific!" he said, the smoke propelled in separate bursts from each nostril. "You have some run-in with Larch that you don't tell us about. You bring into the case some dead old lady we never heard of. And you're *sure* Larch was her killer even though you don't have any proof. Just who was this Mrs. Whitten anyway?"

"Lenny knew her. The manuscript had been in her family."

"I think I better have a look at that thing."

"Sergeant, it's my passport out of Fourth Avenue and into Miami Beach. I'm selling it to some library or college and then I'm heading to the veranda of the Cross Winds Hotel, where I'm gonna sit in a deck chair and never look at another book again."

"Far as I'm concerned, it's evidence. I can have a judge order you to turn it over. We're dealing with a murder case."

"*Was* a murder case," Howard said. "The crime is solved. Pretty soon Larch is going to be frying in the hot seat."

Howard remembered Harry insisting that if all incurable criminals were put to death tomorrow, there were be a lot less crime in the next generation.

England did it in the eighteenth century, he said, and that's why it has a low crime rate today. Crime was bred out of the population. Without a doubt," Harry said, "an Englishman, even at his worse, makes a more comfortable neighbor than a Mississippian or a Texan."

"That's stupid, Harry," Pop answered. "England has a low crime rate because it's never had a bunch of different cultures coming together all at once like we do here. And some of these yo-yos that come here, especially those who talk Spanish, just happen to be a lot more violent than others."

"A point well taken, my bibliographic chum, although you have never seen a more pitiful example of humanity than the hillbillies from our own Appalachian states. Nevertheless, where crime is concerned, the object of punishment should be to simply exterminate the criminal. The easiest and cheapest way of getting rid of the Pretty Boy Floyds and Bonnie and Clydes is to kill them. If we have two thousand executions a year instead of one hundred thirty that would be an enormous improvement. Just think, after the shock of two thousand executions wears off, we'd have two thousand fewer criminals."

A couple of browsers opened the front door and Mulvey came back into focus.

"I gotta get back to work, Sergeant, I got customers. Is there anything else I can do for you?"

"Yeah," Mulvey said, picking up his books from the counter. "I want that manuscript of yours on my desk at the Twenty-third by noon tomorrow."

Mulvey tapped his hat and went out at the same time old man Mandelblatt from next door came in.

"Hey, Howard, you gotta phone call."

Mandelblatt had a phone in his store. Eighty and a half didn't. People who wanted to reach Howard on the phone had to call Mandelblatt. Howard left the browsers on their own and ran next door. Ann Elkin was on the other end of the phone.

"Terrific news, Howard! I just heard from Professor Svalgard. They tested the manuscript leaf you left at Columbia and it *matches*. The paper was made in England between 1780 and 1790! It even has a watermark from the Whitecassel Press of London. Professor Svalgard says that's exactly the kind of paper Coxe would have used in 1790. Aren't you excited, Howard? Now all you have to do is to find a buyer. And Columbia is interested."

He didn't reply.

"Howard? Howard, are you there?"

"Yeah, I'm here."

"There's something wrong, Howard."

"Yeah, Ann. The manuscript. I keep thinking about what Harry was trying to tell me about it."

"What?"

"I still think maybe I laid an egg."

23

He took his familiar route between Patience and Fortitude up the weary steps into the library with the Coxe manuscript, out of sight in its box, under his arm. The sound of his heels on the marble floor flagged his path as he went into the main reading room and looked around for Ann Elkin. She was pushing a cart loaded with books and about to enter the delivery-desk stockade when he caught up with her.

"Ann!"

She turned and saw him. "Shhhhhh," she warned. "Hawksmith's creeping around here somewhere."

"Do you have them?"

"I have them."

She stooped and took three large books from the bottom shelf of the cart. He bent down, almost dropping the Coxe manuscript, and helped her to lift them up, his hand over hers. She opened one of the books and fanned the pages.

"This is a copy of the fourth edition that was printed in 1936, the 1945 supplement, and the 1948 supplement."

"Jesus, they're heavy. Okay, Ann. I'm gonna find a quiet table somewhere and get to work."

"I don't understand why you think it's necessary to read those books, Howard."

"I told you on the phone. The Coxe manuscript. Harry's raised some questions about it."

"Impossible, Howard. He's had a terrible stroke, can't read, can't write, can't communicate. You're not even sure he could *hear* you when you read it to him."

"He told me, Ann."

"But you said yourself, Harry can't talk! You were sitting right across from him in his study."

"He *told* me, Ann. Now I have to find out exactly what he meant."

"Christ, Howard, you've already had it on the best authority that the manuscript's genuine. Professor Svalgard says Columbia wants to buy it. Those books you're holding aren't going to help you anyway. They're about the American language. The Coxe manuscript was written by an *Englishman*. You're wasting your time!"

"Ann—"

"Don't cause more trouble for yourself. Sell the fucking manuscript! Take the money!"

"Harry wouldn't approve." He reached out and touched Ann's hair.

"Watch it!" she hissed. "Here she comes. You've got to scram."

The hawk lady approached them on gimpy bird's feet. She came within inches of Howard's chest and pointed at his chin with her beaklike nose.

"Is there something wrong here, Miss Elkin?" she said. "Young man, may we assist you with something?"

Ann spoke. "It's all right, Miss Hawksmith, I was just helping this gentleman to find a couple of items." Ann turned to Howard. "Do you have what you think you need, sir?"

"Ah, yeah, lady. Thanks."

Ann pushed her cart behind the counter of the delivery desk, giving him a wink. Hawksmith watched him suspiciously as he lugged the books to an isolated seat at the corner of an oak reading table and sat down. He slid the precious manuscript under his chair, opened the first book, and began turning its pages in the yellowish library light. Despite the rows of brass desk lamps with their green shades and the soaring chandeliers containing circles of tiny lights, the library was a dim and gloomy place to work. He wanted a smoke but it was not the spot to light up a Chesterfield. He reached into his jacket pocket and pulled out a pack of Sen-Sen and popped some into his mouth, the licorice flavor hot on his tongue. As he flipped the pages, he saw right away he was going to have trouble. The damned book was so long! And in the back were pages and pages listing words and phrases. The index ran to dozens of more pages. *Supplement I* was the same way and so was the second. He opened *Supplement II* to the preface and read it. Slowly. He was always a slow reader—which is why he never got out of Evander Childs High School in the Bronx.

In the preface, Harry wrote that was he was just a journalist whose hobby was words and so he wasn't trained in linguistic science. Howard was sure that meant something about language. Then Harry wrote he couldn't claim profundity. *Profundity?* Holy shit, Howard thought, if Harry couldn't claim profundity, whatever that was, then why was he trying to read this goddamned book? He snapped it shut. Could be Ann was right. These were books about *American* language and he was trying to find out something, he wasn't sure what, about a manuscript written by some *English* guy in 1790. Didn't make sense.

He looked up at the gilt ceiling far above. It was carved with complicated designs of leaves and circles and swirls and the torsos of naked women. Hubba hubba. The Army-Navy game could have been played under that ceiling with room left over for the cheering squad. Every sound reverberated around the endless rows of tables. Footsteps squeaked, crunched, or clicked on the red-stone floor. A cough was far-off thunder. The scrape of a chair sounded like the screech of a sedan's brakes.

He went back to the first book he had opened and turned to the initial chapter. In the first sentence, Harry wrote that the early American colonists *had* to invent Americanisms if only to describe the unfamiliar landscape, weather, and—Howard wasn't sure what the last two words meant—flora and fauna. Wait a minute, flora meant, like, florists. Flowers. Of course! Fauna he'd heard of but just couldn't remember what it was. Anyway, what Harry said made sense. A guy goes to a strange place and sees something he's never seen before, he's gotta give it a name just so's he can talk about it. The colonists had to do that so they could communicate to each other about the sights in the New World.

He turned the page and read some more. Harry quoted a Dr. Johnson who, in the 1700s, hated anything American and called their words vile and intolerable. Screw you, buddy. He read on about Daniel Webster (or was it Noah?). Hell, even Howard knew about Webster. He wrote all those dictionaries. They even named an avenue for him in the Bronx. Webster saw that English was going through a lot of changes in America in both pronunciation and vocabulary and was willing to go along with them even though he wasn't happy about it.

Then Harry quoted some English captain, a Thomas Hamilton, who complained about what he called American barbarisms, saying they weren't confined to the ignorant but also came from the lips of the learned. Howard thumbed through the pages until he landed in a section in which Harry referred to a John Pickering who wrote a book in 1816 called *A Vocabulary or Collection of Words and Phrases Which Have Been Supposed to be Peculiar to the United States*. Catchy title. Pickering broke down Americanisms into three categories. New words formed in America, words still used in England to which Americans have given new meanings, and other words that are obsolete in England but still in common use in America. Howard began to get dizzy. He hadn't done so much studying since he was in the eighth grade.

He marked his place in Harry's book with a matchbook and stood up and stretched, then went to the john. He stood there looking down into the urinal and trying to put some meaning into all he'd learned so far. So far, nothing was coming through. He flushed the john, watching the water swirl around a cake of pungent-smelling paraffin.

He returned to his seat at the library table, found his bookmark, put the matches back into his pocket, and read on. Harry wrote that the first Americanisms were words borrowed from the Indians and later the Dutch, the Spanish, and the other countries that colonized America. The early settlers freely interchanged the parts of speech by turning nouns into verbs and verbs into nouns and adjectives into either or both without rhyme or reason. Howard never was able to tell the difference between a verb and an adverb even though Miss Brockstein kept him in seventh-grade English for three years in a row.

Other new words were created by changing the meaning of the original English versions. Then a lot of those American-style words started sneaking back into England. No wonder the upper-class English got uppity when they heard them. Some words that the English denounced as American barbarisms were actually archaic English words that held on in isolated parts of America like the Appalachian Mountains or the Maine coast or eastern North Carolina. Americans started inventing their own words, sometimes mysteriously, as they moved west, so that nobody today knows how or why a lot of them were formed.

He put the book down and picked up *Supplement II*. In it, Harry wrote that nine-tenths of the English vocabulary was safely buried in the dictionaries and that there was evidence that the language could be spoken intelligibly with fewer than one thousand words. Howard had never counted but he was sure he didn't have half that many words in his own vocabulary. He went on to read Harry's opinion that English, which had constantly changed over the centuries, probably would go right on changing as it spread over the world. That didn't seem to bother Harry, who also insisted that he preferred American English over Standard English. American was better, he concluded, because it was clearer, more rational, and best of all, more charming. Howard closed the book.

So what now, he wondered?

Reference books of all shapes and sizes lined the walls, even extending to a narrow mezzanine overlooking the room. There were the various books of who's who, volumes listing the officers of the

Army of the United States from 1779 on, encyclopedias of American and English biography, telephone books for every city in the nation, wildlife encyclopedias, dictionaries of plant names, even *The North American Yatch Register*.

He reached into his coat pocket and pulled out the list of words he had copied down in Harry's study at 1524 Hollins Street. Maybe the best thing to do would be to look each one up in Harry's index and see what the Sage had to say about it. He opened the piece of paper on the desk. Then he hauled the Coxe manuscript from under his chair and took it out of its box. The first word Harry seemed to question was *to*. That was innocent enough. Everyone uses *to*. He read the sentence in the Coxe manuscript:

I had been to Paris twice the previous fall and I was quite familiar with its fortifications, not to mention its many stores, cafes, and places of revelry.

There were two *to*s in the sentence, but he was pretty sure Harry had stopped him on the first one. He turned to Harry's index and found a listing for *to* and went to it. The guy named Pickering that Harry had quoted, the one who wrote that book on American English in 1816, cited *to* as an Americanism and gave an example. Americans would say "I have been *to* Philadelphia, while the English would say "I have been *in* or *at* Philadelphia." Shit, so what? Little word like that!

The next word on the list was *fall*. He looked it up in Harry's tome. It was an archaic word the English had long replaced with *autumn*. The Americans kept on using *fall*. Harry quoted a couple of English scholars who condemned Americanisms in 1906. They told their countrymen that Americanisms were not only foreign words but should be treated like foreign words even though some, like *fall*, did have their good side, being short, accurate, and to the point.

He started breathing heavily as he looked up the next word, *stores*. Now what the hell could possibly be wrong with that? A lot, it turned out. Harry explained that *store* was one of the new

American words of the colonial period, a transformation of the English *shop*. In fact, the first known use of *store* for *shop* appeared in an American publication issued in 1721. By 1741 the word was expanded to *storekeeper*, while in England, even now, the word *store* meant a large establishment, like a warehouse.

Holy shit. What was next? *Cafe*. He looked it up. A so-called "loan word," from France, an American term for a drinking place, traced to 1893. *1893?* The word hadn't even been around when Coxe wrote his piece in 1790.

He began to perspire in the overheated library room as he went back to the manuscript.

The people of Paris were in a mood for insurrection and there had twice been near-engagements with troops under the marshal de Broglio following the plan of the duke of Coigny who had distributed his forces around the capitol.

Near-engagements. Next word on the list. He turned to it in Harry's book. A lot of words using *near-* started to appear about 1900, he learned. Like *near-silk*, or *near-silver*. A logical extension was *near-accident* or *near-smile*. So, *near-engagement* was a word that *nobody* used in the eighteenth Century, not even the Americans. He turned to the manuscript again.

He had crowded his infantry into three or four little camps on natural ponds near the city; his cavalry occupied two well-planned parks in Grenelle and St. Denys, and his large artillery arrived in the later place.

Pond. He found it. In the late 1830s, James Fenimore Cooper complained about an American tendency to abuse certain terms, such as *pond* for *lake* and *park* for *square*. In fact, Harry pointed out that *pond* began to be used in place of natural *lake* in America as early as 1622. The English sometimes used *pond* but only to refer to a small artificial pool.

I do not mean to moralize but had I been in command my first movement would have been to ensure the person of Louis XVI.

The American War did not form great generals among the French and while I do not wish to belittle the young men employed in it, it should be said that they had the opportunity of examining a new people who were governed by an influential constitution.

Moralize. Influential. Belittle. Not all American inventions but words violently denounced by eighteenth-century English purists.

The heads of the French troops had been made giddy by those backwoodsmen.

Backwoodsman. An Americanism traced to 1784. But would an educated Englishman like William Trevor Coxe have used it, or even heard of it, in 1790?

He closed Harry's book, put it aside, and carefully returned the manuscript to its box. Then he sat back in his chair and looked up at the ceiling, so high it seemed to be veiled by haze. Well, Harry, he thought, you knew the language all right. Even Professor Svalgard didn't pick up on it. One thing was sure, whoever wrote *An Englishman's Account of the Revolution of 1789 and the Taking of the Bastille* wasn't an Englishman. And whoever it was had scribbled it in the twentieth century. Howard didn't have to graduate Evander Childs High School in the Bronx to figure that out. Then he remembered something. Fauna. Animal life! That's what it meant. In the same way that flora meant plant life.

Maybe Pop had underestimated Howard's intelligence. Maybe he wasn't so dumb after all. He was no brain but he had still been able to figure out what Harry was trying to communicate in that hot room on Hollins Street. Now all he had to do was to find out who had taken Lenny and him to the cleaners.

He felt a finger tapping him on the shoulder. He looked up. It was Ann.

"Howard, I have awful news!"

Her face was white.

"What happened?"

"The police just called. It's Larch. He's *escaped* from the Tombs! And he's got a gun."

24

It was up to Ronald Newberry now. He was Howard's last hope of finding out how he and Lenny got rooked. The Coxe manuscript was a dud. Everything was gone. All the money. Lenny. He didn't have enough dough to pay Klein the landlord or the good old First National. Klein was sure to throw him out. The landlady who rented him his room on West 181st Street would do the same. Ann Elkin, who had put up with him for four years, wasn't able to bail him out. Following Pop to Florida was a failed dream. To make matters worse, Larch was at large again. But this time, it didn't matter, Howard thought. Larch could *have* the goddamned Coxe manuscript. It wasn't worth nothing.

He read the ads over the windows of the number 4 train as it rumbled to Grand Central. The St. James Theater was home to *Where's Charley* with Ray Bolger. John Wanamakers on Liberty Street was selling forty-five-dollar suits. Polish hams were $1.59 a pound at the A&P. Pan Am was flying passengers to London in less than fourteen hours. Hoagy Carmichael was sitting at a piano holding a bottle of Schaefer Beer. The train screeched to its stop in a shower of sparks. He got off and walked with the crowds through the tunnels and stairways to Forty-second Street, where a cop was dangling his nightstick and humming "Nature Boy." He was beginning to hate that damned song.

He turned north at Madison to Newberry's gallery on Forty-ninth. Copies of his book on collecting were still neatly displayed in a semicircle in the window. Didn't look like there was a lot of demand for it. Maybe he gave it away to his clients. *He* had clients. *Howard* had customers. The bell chimed as he opened the front door and stepped inside. Newberry had a damned small inventory. Not like 80½, which was crammed floor to ceiling with ratty volumes. Newberry kept a few leather editions placed in decorative positions in cabinets here and there, bound manuscripts artfully displayed on end tables. On a mahogany stand was a bust of some ancient Greek-looking guy labeled PALLAS. Expensive prints in even more expensive frames hung on the walls. On Fourth Avenue, books, not pictures, claimed the wall space. With all that artwork and the leather sofa and the French chairs, Howard could have been in the outer office of some executive at Morgan's Bank down on Wall Street, begging for another loan. Some violin music came from a speaker somewhere and it wasn't playing *Bei Mir Bist Du Schön*. He didn't see anyone.

"Newberry? Miss Kelly?" he called.

There was no answer. They must have been in the back room. Careless of them to leave those expensive books and manuscripts unsupervised, he thought. Some wino could come in from the street and make off with a Washington or a Franklin or the bust of Pallas (whoever he was).

"Newberry?" he called again. "Miss Kelly?"

Suddenly, Kelly's head poked out from behind the curtain that separated the back room from the main store.

"Oh, it's you," she said. She seemed a little flustered. A few strands of her hair fell over her forehead.

"Yeah, I came to see Mr. Newberry."

"I'm not sure—"

"It's about this manuscript we talked about."

"I'm afraid it's too late—"

"You don't understand. There's something I gotta find out."

He walked toward her. She quickly came out and stood in front of the curtain to bar his way.

"Mr. Newberry cannot see you now. You'll have to go."

"Well, hell, then I'll just wait."

He had brought the box with the Coxe manuscript, so he threw it down on the Queen Anne desk. There was a low cabinet next to it, so he shoved some books aside and flopped down on it.

"Please, Mr. Howard, the credenza."

"Huh?"

"You are sitting on an eighteenth-century credenza. Please!"

"Please *yourself,* girlie. I been through too much and I gotta have a few words with your boss."

"For the last time—"

Then he heard Newberry's voice from behind the drape. "Is something wrong, Miss Kelly?" He stuck his head out. His face was red.

"Mr. Howard, may I do something for you?"

He stepped around the curtain. His tie was a little askew. Maybe he and Kelly had been having a go at it.

"Yeah, this is the manuscript everyone's been so goddammed interested in," Howard said, removing the lid from the box. "Take a look at it."

Newberry stepped to the desk and turned a few pages of the manuscript without taking it out of the box.

"Ah, indeed, the Coxe manuscript. I suppose you are here to try and sell it."

"It's a fake, Mr. Newberry."

"You sound very sure of yourself. I suppose you determined that bit of information all by yourself?"

"I had a little help."

"Well, if that's the case, Mr. Howard, I certainly don't know what you want of me. I have no interest in fakes and forgeries. I run a legitimate business here."

"I'm trying to get some idea how Lenny and I got cheated on this thing. And I think you hold the key. Lenny said the manuscript came from a collection owned by a Mrs. Gertrude Whitten on Riverside Drive. You know Mrs. Whitten, don't you?"

"Certainly not. Mrs. Whitten passed away months ago. But I do know her son-in-law, Dr. Liebknecht of Mount Sinai Hospital. He's the executor of her estate and in closing her apartment, he sold her collection to me. There was no such manuscript in her library. In fact, there was very little of value. There *was* a substantial collection of first editions by the nineteenth-century New England poets but that was about all. I paid more than I should have for that library and got very little in return."

"But Lenny said that—"

"I cannot help what Lenny said. Now, Mr. Howard, you must go. I have an important client waiting."

"*Why don't you tell him the truth, goddammit?*" Larch burst through the curtain and into the room. He was holding a gun, much larger than the little silver weapon that he used to pistol-whip Howard. He wore a tan topcoat, unbuttoned to show prison dungarees. Larch put the gun against Newberry's head. The book dealer's crooked eyes were like beacon lights gone haywire.

Kelly began to sob.

"Shaddup, lady, you're in this, too. Okay, Newberry, tell him."

"May I sit down, Mr. Larch?" Newberry asked. Dots of perspiration rose on his forehead.

"Sit. You, too, lady."

Newberry pulled his pants legs up slightly to preserve the crease and sat on a French chair across from the desk. Kelly took a seat some feet away by the bust of that Pallas guy.

"I guess I have no choice but to tell you, Mr. Howard," Newberry said. "It's really a case of a falling-out among thieves." His hand trembled as he reached into the inside pocket of his suit, pulled a Gauloise from its case, and lighted it with his gold lighter. "We had no idea it would lead to murder, but it did. As you know, Mr. Larch here has been highly successful in running down special volumes and manuscripts. On demand. Because certain conditions made it difficult for Mr. Larch to operate openly himself, he came to me. It seemed to be a mutually beneficial arrangement. I gave him a want list of books desired among my very select clientele. Mr. Larch was skilled in meeting that demand. As time went on, we happened to acquire original papers contemporary with various periods of our history."

Newberry stopped and dragged on his cigarette.

"Go on. Tell him how we did it," growled Larch.

"Well, ah, frequently, we simply removed blank leaves from old books whose value would be much less than a document written by, say, Benjamin Franklin. Of course, it is doubtful that a letter from a statesman or literary figure of the past would have been written on a leaf obviously cut from a book. Thanks to Mr. Larch and his unique abilities to get behind locked doors, we discovered an almost endless supply and variety of antique paper stock at the New England Paper Institute of Concord, New Hampshire, a treasure trove of paper made by early-American paper mills. The Institute still doesn't know their sample papers are missing. Mr. Larch left plenty behind."

"Tell him about the watermarks," Larch said.

"Oh yes. We learned to identify the age of the papers through the watermarks, a tricky business since certain devious Continental papermakers often duplicated the watermark of the highly regarded Whatman paper mill, established in Maidstone, England, in 1731. You see, I know what I am talking about."

"And the inks," prompted Larch.

"Indeed, our inks were uncanny duplicates of the original inks, based on the ink formulas of the time. For example, early inks would bite into the paper, showing an almost invisible brownness at the edges of the pen strokes. Because of the iron content in early inks, some inks used before 1875 would show a slight corrosion. Naturally, I consulted with chemists, as any enterprising dealer of my stature would be expected to do. The science being learned, it occurred to us that we could supplement our business with documents and manuscripts written to order. That's really about it."

"Not quite," Larch said, prodding Newberry's head with the gun barrel. "Tell him about the other guy."

Newberry removed a handkerchief that had been folded to a point from the breast pocket of his coat and dabbed at his forehead. "Neither Mr. Larch nor myself, nor Miss Kelly here, were particularly adept at forging words and signatures ourselves," Newberry said, "but we luckily happened onto someone who had the ability, a person who had studied calligraphy and penmanship."

"Explain why this guy was good," Larch demanded.

"It seems, inept forgers rarely master the handwriting of their subjects. Frequently, their handwriting is shaky or shows evidence of being traced. And above all, the clumsy forger's handwriting is often noticeably small, perhaps because of some inward guilt. We were careful to avoid those pitfalls."

Newberry paused and cleared his throat.

"Go on, go on," ordered Larch, "tell him about the guy."

"I'm getting to that. Even more than the physical execution of a fake manuscript or document, we had to focus on the content. It had to be consistent with the nature and history of the person supposed to have penned it. Small errors of date or place would give it away. There could be no references to inventions or events or books that came after the date the document was to have been written. Bad grammar or misspellings would not, for example, be typical of a manuscript by Longfellow or Emerson. A letter by Lincoln would have to be identical to his spare, almost terse writing style. And Lincoln never signed his name 'Abe.' Washington's signature is bold and curvaceous, not tentative and cramped."

Newberry put out his cigarette in a crystal ashtray.

"Get on with it," Larch said.

"Frankly, Mr. Howard, we were *good*," Newberry said. We stuck to what we knew. *Americana*. We began to bring forward the lost literature and history of our past. Unrecorded treasures eagerly sought by private collectors. A real service when one thinks about it. A way of giving joy and of illuminating history."

Larch laughed.

Howard thumped his fist on the desk. "I don't know how you can say that, Newberry. Screwing up history is what you've done, *not* illuminating it. You've fooled people into thinking certain things happened as history when they didn't. I don't know how many of those forgeries you've passed around but my guess is you've fucked up scholarship for years."

Newberry nervously lighted another cigarette. "Tidbits of history, that's all. Not really enough to damage the reach of scholarship, I assure you."

Larch began pacing, waving his gun. "Finish it up, Newberry, dammit," he said. "I told you to tell him about the guy."

Newberry coughed slightly. "Well, after a while, Miss Kelly and I found it increasingly difficult to work with our friend Mr. Larch here and his somewhat unpredictable temper. To describe it simply, we wanted to back out of our arrangement with him. But there was a complicating factor. A fourth person." He inhaled on the cigarette and blew the smoke out his nose.

"Tell him!" Larch demanded.

Newberry cleared his throat. "I'm afraid your friend Mr. Gould wasn't all he appeared to be."

"*Lenny?*"

"Not only was Mr. Gould a student of history, he was, as you know, a student of calligraphy. And a good one."

"You mean *Lenny?*" Howard started to leave his seat. Larch pointed the gun in his direction. Howard sat back down.

"Correct, Mr. Howard," Newberry said. "Lenny was our forger."

"And the Coxe manuscript . . ."

Newberry waved his cigarette, his fingers trembling. "I'm afraid Lenny got a little carried away with that one. After it was composed, I wasn't sure we could quite pull it off. You see, to forge a document, you have to think like the person supposed to have written it. Now, it's one thing to think like an American, even though the America of our past was only in a *few* ways like the America of today. Almost a different country, in fact. But to think like a well-bred, upper-class Englishman of the eighteenth century, and a military man, as well! Lenny believed he could do it, though. He felt he knew enough about the French Revolutionary period. It was his speciality. I wasn't convinced. Still, the created document *was* remarkable. In appearance, it was a masterpiece of deception. The scholarship seemed absolutely authentic. However, I was afraid there might have been other factors, hardly noticeable to any but the most exacting scholar, that might give it away."

"The language," Howard said. "Not English enough."

Newberry shrugged. "The language appeared authentic."

"Not enough for my friend Harry, wise guy. That's how I found out it was a fake!"

"At any rate, I absolutely barred its sale. Just too risky. Then Lenny had an idea."

"What?"

"*You.* He would sell it to you. On his own. That would keep the Newberry Gallery out of it. The manuscript would be virtually untraceable since purportedly it came from the estate of Mrs. Whitten, who at that time plainly had only days or weeks to live. But obviously there would have been no record of the manuscript as part of the Whitten estate. Lenny, Mr. Larch, Miss Kelly, and I would divide the cash. Not a large sum, but our many smaller transactions have kept us in the high-rent district. You would have the manuscript and if you were to have sold it, fine. If it escaped detection as a fake, that was fine, too. If, however, it was identified for what it was, then it would be you who would have to repay the money you received and face the risk of possible legal action. That would have been too bad. For you."

"I can't believe Lenny would do that to me. You, I could believe it. But Lenny!"

Newberry stubbed out his cigarette in the crystal ashtray. "*That* was your Lenny all right. He was bright enough and I would have used him further, educated him further, if he had kept his nose clean. But he wanted to take greater chances. Bigger risks. Concoct documents that created a larger threat of being unmasked. He became very demanding. Pushy, you might say."

"Lenny could be that way," Howard agreed.

"Then Lenny began implying that he might have to expose our little racket if we didn't play ball with him."

"So," Howard said, turning to Larch, "you went to Lenny's apartment that night and killed him. Under orders from Newberry here."

"That's not true, shithead!" Larch said, pacing the floor. He was perspiring heavily. "I went to his room all right. But to get the manuscript, not to kill him. I had a better deal going. Not the miserable four grand you were offering. I stood to double that amount by selling it to Harvard. Harvard! I'd already approached the people who ran its special collections. Pseudonymously, of course. There was a good chance I'd get away with it. I was about to take Lenny in as a partner. Use him as my front. Dump this chicken-livered Newberry and his girlfriend. All right, so now the Harvard deal's out the window. But I needed the Coxe manuscript anyway and at last you brought it to me on a silver platter. That's the proof that'll make Newberry burn, *not* me! Because I know where New-berry keeps the papers and the ink used to make that fake."

Larch turned his back on Kelly as he spoke. Out of the corner of his eye, Howard saw her stealthily get up from her chair and put her arms around the bust of Pallas. Either she was stronger than she looked for a skinny lady or the bust was lighter than it seemed. She raised the statue shoulder-high and then hurled it at Larch.

"Nevermore!" she shouted as the bust smashed into Larch's head and shoulders, the statue breaking into a hundred pieces when it hit the floor. The impact propelled Larch forward, the gun whirling from his hand. Both Newberry and Howard leaped up at the same time, grabbing for the gun, which was spinning on the floor like a top. They careened into a stand, knocking to the floor what may have been a priceless Washington manuscript but that, knowing Newberry, probably wasn't priceless and probably wasn't even a Washington. Newberry got to the gun first but Howard's hand was on top of Newberry's hand a second later. They rolled on the floor, wrestling for the weapon.

"Give it to me, you fool," Howard shouted. "He's a murderer! He'll kill us."

Larch groaned and began trying to get to his feet.

"Get the gun, Ronald! Get the gun!" Kelly screamed.

Suddenly Howard got Newberry's elbow in his face. Against his cheekbone. Hard. Then again. His hearing aid was jolted from his ear and skittered on the floor, the cord pulling along the battery from his coat pocket. Howard tried to twist Newberry's hand off of the stock of the gun. With the fingernails of his other hand, Newberry began to claw at his opponent. It was too much. Howard was battered. He had never been a tough guy anyway. Newberry got the gun, shoved Howard away, rose to a crouching position, and fired two shots at Larch. The explosions might have been deafening to anyone but Howard, who was just a couple of feet away. But without his hearing aid, they were just like pops. The bullets apparently missed their target but shattered a framed print on the wall behind Larch.

Larch ducked around the desk, then over the top of the leather sofa. Newberry got off another shot. Larch screamed in pain from behind the sofa. Then a small cabinet came flying over the top of the sofa almost directly at Newberry. It was one of those credenzas. The eighteenth-century one. It splintered as it hit the floor and, startled, Newberry lost his balance.

For a big man, Larch moved faster than Howard would have thought. He ran from the side of the sofa, trying to keep the various chairs and tables between him and Newberry, who struggled to his feet and fired a fourth shot. By this time, Larch was at the end of the room and dived feet first through Newberry's plate-glass window, showering the sidewalk in front with shards of glass, and toppling Newberry's carefully arranged display of *Collecting the Rare and the Beautiful*. Newberry fired two more shots. Larch rose to his feet and started to run west toward Fifth Avenue, holding his arm, which was dripping blood.

"We got to catch him!" Howard screamed. "Come on, Newberry! Kelly, you call the cops."

"Don't move!" Newberry ordered. The gun was pointed at Howard's chest. "The police will be here shortly but you won't."

"What do you mean?"

"Because Larch will have killed you."

"What are you talking about, Newberry. That goddamned guy's a murderer."

"No, *he's* not the murderer."

Newberry's finger tightened around the trigger. Howard knew that a bullet was about to fly from the revolver into his chest, a bullet so fast he wouldn't be able to see it, only a flash from the barrel, a puff of smoke. He'd faintly hear the sound of the shot and then excruciating pain. And then. Nothing. He would be nothing.

> "Death is such good-news," Harry said, "especially for the mortician whose profession has been slowed by the progress of medical science. Death by a bullet is an affront to one's dignity, but in due course, a sure, safe, easy, and sanitary means of leaving this vale will be invented. A pity, though, that death by shooting is such an inefficient means of extermination. Why, are you aware of the positive benefits of the black plague? It launched the Renaissance by eliminating such huge masses of peasants that the intelligence and industriousness of the European race were raised incalculably. Until that time, the intelligentsia had been hobbled from below. Before the black plague, the best minds of Europe had their hands full attending to the wasteful activity of politics, taking new territories from one another, keeping the proletariat in line. The best thing about the black plague was that it killed selectively, wiping out the masses but keeping intact most of the upper-class population. Yes, my dear bookseller, a bullet in the chest is increasingly a more fashionable way to die. But soooo inefficient."

"Harry!" Howard cried. "I wanna wait for the black plague. Save me!"

"Who's Harry?" Newberry said, one puzzled eye looking east, the other west.

"Never mind! Do it!" Kelly shouted. "Shoot the bastard!"

"But who's Harry?"

"Pull the trigger, *asshole!*" Kelly screamed.

Newberry's finger tightened around the trigger. The hammer strained slowly backward and then sprang forward. If he hadn't lost his hearing aid, Howard might have heard a faint click. A click! Not a shot.

Newberry pulled the trigger again and again.

"Harry!" Howard yelled. "Thanks!"

He didn't wait for Newberry to pull the trigger of the empty gun another time. From the floor, Howard scooped up the batteries from his hearing aid and flung them into Newberry's face. The impact knocked Newberry back a few steps as Howard jumped through the hole in the plate-glass window and landed on his feet on Forty-ninth Street.

"Who the fuck is Harry?" Newberry yelled, his hand at his bleeding nose. He threw the worthless weapon after Howard. It hit the sidewalk and split open.

25

He could see small drops of blood, bright on the sidewalk. Larch had left an easy trail at first. Big crowds swarmed around Saks Fifth Avenue. That's where he lost the scent, any blood on the sidewalk obscured by the soles of thousands of shoes. He wasn't sure which way Larch might have run. The big man could have gone into Rockefeller Center, losing himself among the crowds watching the ice skaters. He might have headed north to Central Park and the zoo and the carousel. But then Howard realized that, no, Larch would only go south. To where the books were. The library. His chest heaving, he pushed on down Fifth Avenue, buffeting the crowds going in the opposite direction. He ducked around the cars as he crossed Forty-second Street, then started up the steps of the library.

As he got to Fortitude, he stopped and leaned against the lion to catch his breath. It was then that he noticed the blood. A smear of it along the side of the statue. It was the same place Larch had leaned to catch *his* breath. Howard lumbered up the steps and went through the bronze doorway into the huge lobby. Which way, he wondered? Then he knew it could only be one way. The third floor. The main reading room. The Bottom Collection. He ran up the north stairs three flights, through the rotunda, and into the catalog room. It was there that despite the loss of his hearing aid, he heard loud voices. A commotion.

Larch was there all right. Confronted by Miss Hawksmith, her tiny frame intimidating his more-than-six-foot bulk.

"I tell you, young man, this is a library and you are disturbing it."

It was happening just outside the cage of the delivery desk. Where Ann worked.

"I shall have you arrested, young man, if you persist."

Larch moved a step or two backward as she prodded his chest with a crooked finger, the nail cut very short.

"Furthermore," she said, "you are bleeding on my floor. I won't have that. This is a library, I'll have you know. People don't bleed here!" He backed farther away from the old bird, around the main desk of the catalog room, and out into the rotunda where Howard was standing, wheezing from the exertion of running down Fifth Avenue and the three-story climb.

"Larch!" Howard said.

Larch turned around unsteadily. Fear was on his face. The fight had gone out of him.

"It's all right, Larch, it's me. Howard. I know you didn't kill Lenny."

Howard stepped toward him. Larch began to move backward, then he realized Hawksmith was behind him. There seemed to be no place to run. He was a huge man but he was trapped like the smallest of animals, cornered by a half-deaf bookseller and a slight old lady. And by his many misdeeds.

"Larch," Howard said, "I want to help you."

Larch turned to his left and ran through the rotunda and down a short flight of stairs to a landing. A large window, open, overlooked an inner courtyard. Below, there might have been a few cars, a wheelbarrow, some tools. But the ground was paved with concrete. Hard, cold concrete. Painfully Larch pulled himself up to the windowsill. Howard ran down the steps but stopped abruptly when he heard Larch shout.

"*Stay where you are!*"

"Larch," Howard pleaded. "Everyone knows you're a crook. *You* admit it. But you're no murderer. Climb down from that window. We'll get you to a hospital. Take care of that arm. Mulvey will throw out the murder charge. You'll go to jail but you won't *burn.*"

"I've had it. I can't take anymore. I'm going to jump!"

"Larch, listen to me. It's not that bad. A couple of years in Sing Sing and you'll be out. You'll be able to start up your book business again. Legitimate. It's Newberry and Kelly. They're the ones who are gonna fry."

Howard moved forward a little.

Larch shrank back, leaning out of the window, his hands holding on to the frame, ready to let go. "Stay away from me, dammit. I'm going to do it!"

"Larch, you've made a lot of mistakes, had a lot of bad luck. But it's not too late. Things will change. For the better!"

Larch turned his head and looked down at the courtyard three stories below.

"I'm going! This is it."

"Young man!" It was the voice of Miss Hawksmith.

She pushed Howard aside.

"Whatever are you doing in that window?"

"I, I . . ." Larch stammered.

"Climb down!"

"No! I'm going to—"

"Not in *my* library. I said to *climb down!*"

"But . . ."

"I said to *climb down!*"

Larch oozed to the marble floor like a glob of blubber, his head thumping against the wall. He was out. Life had never gone too well for Richard James Larch.

"The nerve of that young man! Someone pick him up and show him out!" demanded Hawksmith.

26

Howard felt a hand on his arm. Soft.

"Is it over?" she asked. It was Ann Elkin.

"It's over," he said.

Her breath mingled with his own. She had had onion soup for lunch.

> Now Harry was philosophic about women. He complained that nowhere but in America did women have more leisure and freedom to improve their minds, and nowhere else was there worse cooking in the home. The land of the emancipated woman was also the land of canned food, he said.
>
> "Emancipated woman or not," Howard said, "for me it's a matter of love."
>
> "Love!" Harry said. "That's a phenomenon best cured by marriage."
>
> "But . . ."
>
> "The girl who was perfect in her wedding dress soon becomes a slattern in a moth-eaten bathrobe. By the same token, the bridegroom, so debonair in his best suit, turns into a shambling, driveling nuisance in worn-out pajamas. The only thing that saves marriage is habit and regularity. The couple gets used to the sights and smells in the same way that they become accustomed to the odor and noise from the glue factory down the block."
>
> "Harry, Ann Elkin is so pretty. Her dark hair. Her bangs. Her gams. Her small feet. Smooth hands."
>
> "So you think she's pretty, do you?"
>
> "She's beautiful!"

"Women, excepting some dime-store slut who is gaga over some phony with a mustache on the silver screen, rarely look for beauty in men. Why should men seek beauty in women? In fact, the human body is not a beautiful thing. The female body in particular is defective, with its harsh curves and its awkwardly distributed masses. Compared to a woman's body, a milk jar or a cuspidor is a thing of beauty. Look at a woman from the side and what do you see?"

"Well, I . . ."

"She looks like a drunken dollar sign!"

"Now wait a minute, Harry, there are other considerations. Men need women to appreciate them."

"Absurd, dear merchant. It is my opinion that nine-tenths of all normal men would carry on all the activities in which they currently engage if there was not a woman in the world. Men work because they want to eat, and it's silly to think that men engage in creative endeavors only to appease an audience, that audience being composed of women. Men want the respect of their fellow craftsmen, not of women. Can you imagine a good doctor putting the opinion of his wife above that of his fellow doctors?"

"The fact is, Harry, men need, well, s-e-x."

"You do not have to spell it, sir. I am hardly shocked by the term."

"And since birth-control devices and abortions are against the law, the only way out is marriage."

"Poppycock, my book-selling friend. There is always the lady of joy. Prostitution is one of the most attractive occupations open to women. And I have found, in my role as a journalist of course, that the prostitute genuinely likes her work and would not trade places with a waitress or a shopgirl. After all, the prostitute has less work to do, finds her job less monotonous, and meets a far greater variety of men."

Ann shook his arm. "Howard, are you all right? Wake up. Look at me, Howard!"

He blinked his eyes.

"Are you sure it's over?" she asked again.

"It's over," he said once more.

27

Well, not quite over.

Mulvey was chewing on a toothpick, leaning against the counter of 80½. A dust ball clung to the elbow of his jacket.

"I guess you guys wanna know the latest," he said.

Ann Elkin sat on the counter holding a Dixie cup filled with Scotch. From his stool, Howard poured Mulvey a drink. And then he splashed one for myself.

"Don't pour me a drink, dammit!" It was Jacob Bluestein.

"Sorry." Howard poured some Scotch into a cup and Bluestein angrily snatched it out of his hand.

"Yes, Sergeant, how did all of this trouble come about?" Ann asked. She brought her drink to her lips.

Mulvey lit a Lucky.

"Well, Newberry and Kelly knew that their racket was being put in jeopardy with Lenny Gould still in the picture. Lenny's standards weren't quite as high as theirs and they knew that sooner or later they'd get caught. Lenny was already branching out on his own, so to speak, by selling Mr. Howard here—"

"No, it's not Mr—"

"—this bogus manuscript. Also, the relationship between Larch and Newberry and Kelly wasn't working out. Larch was intelligent okay but he didn't have their style, their poise. He had a violent streak. He took too many risks. That too threatened Newberry and Kelly's con. So they wanted to break off the marriage. Larch was aware of that, of course. In fact, he had indicated that he was about to enter into some sort of partnership with Lenny and, indeed, let it slip to Newberry and Kelly he was going to visit Lenny that night to talk about the phony Coxe manuscript, the night of the murder. For Newberry and Kelly, it was perfect. Getting rid of two bad birds with one stone. It didn't take much to strangle Lenny. You know how skinny he was. Kelly was a lot stronger than she looked. She did the actual killing. The two of them hung Lenny's body in the bathroom. Larch was their patsy. When he showed up and was discovered in Lenny's room, who could have thought that anyone but Larch would have committed the murder? What Newberry and Kelly didn't know, of course, was that Larch knew where they kept their collection of old paper and period inks. Larch realized that if he could get hold of the manuscript, he could save himself because the document could be linked directly to those old papers and inks and therefore to the real killers. That's why he went after you, Mr. Howard. Newberry and Kelly also needed that manuscript to protect their asses and that's why they were willing to pay you such a good price for it."

"Newberry and Kelly also didn't know about Harry," Howard said.

"Harry?"

"He's the guy who really broke this case."

"Oh yeah? I'd like to talk to him."

"I'm afraid that won't be possible."

"Forget it, Sergeant," Ann said. "Howard's dreaming. He has a fixation on someone who can't move or talk."

Mulvey held out his cup for a refill and Howard sloshed the Scotch in.

"By the way," Mulvey said, "it was Larch's girlfriend who smuggled the thirty-eight into the Tombs. That's how Larch was able to escape. We caught her in Philly. Some woman named Betty. She'll do up to five years."

"Sergeant," Ann said, "don't you have something for Howard, something we talked about earlier?"

"Oh yeah," he said, taking a swig of Scotch, then wiping his mouth with the back of his hand. He put the cup on the counter and reached into the inside pocket of his suit coat and pulled out an envelope.

"This check is for four grand. Now, I only make less than eight grand, so to me that's a hell of a lot of dough."

The detective handed the envelope to Howard, who took out the check and held it up to the light.

"It's yours," Mulvey said, "the money you put together to buy that phony manuscript. It's all there, except we had to convert the cash to a check. Policy of the City of New York, the Honorable William O'Dwyer, Mayor. I'd give you the argyle sock that went with the money, except some joker in the property clerk's office lost it. Or maybe they're wearing it."

"Mulvey—"

"Shit, it's fair."

"Let me buy you another drink Sergeant," said Jacob Bluestein, who spilled some more Scotch into Mulvey's cup.

They were getting drunker by the minute.

There was a cat sound.

Brummell.

Jacob poured some Scotch into the cat's bowl. Brummell hissed at the Scotch. Then he turned at Jacob and hissed at him. The tumor on Brummell's head had grown bigger. He pushed his pink tongue into the Scotch and began to lick it up. The animal liked it.

"And *I* have wonderful news!" Ann said, raising her drink. "About my novel."

Howard shrank on his stool.

"My editor at Macmillan, Edgar Ardery, loves it. Absolutely *adores it!*"

"You get some green up front, Ann?" Howard asked.

"Well, not yet. Obviously not. He wants to me to alter the locale.

"The what?"

"Locale. Instead of California, it's going to be . . . Guess?" They all looked at each other and shook their heads.

"Hawaii!"

"Hawaii?" Mulvey, Bluestein, and Howard all said it at the same time. Brummell looked up from his booze.

"What a brilliant idea Edgar has," Ann said. "I'm going to start with a long description of how the earth that became Hawaii was formed, the volcanic eruptions, the pull of the moon, the impact of the ocean. Then the earliest and most primitive flora and fauna. After that, the first natives, the European explorers. But my *real* heroine will be Lana, an exotic woman of Japanese and European extraction, who owns a brothel in Honolulu but who becomes the Islands' most powerful woman by cornering the pineapple trade. Her story centers on her torn loves for three men: the one who fights his way to become the island's governor; another, a ship's captain who battles pirates between Honolulu and San Francisco; and the last, a courageous doctor who struggles against a yellow-fever epidemic that claims thousands of lives. What do you think?"

The warm Scotch barely disguised their discomfort.

"Ann," Howard said, "I think I read that book already."

"You big palooka! You don't read." Her eyes blazed. "You only sell the things!"

Her drink splattered in his face. He recalled that Harry hated to waste good booze.

> "If it's marriage you insist on, sir, I have one last thing to say to you."
>
> "What, Harry?"
>
> "Just remember that no married man is sincerely happy if he has to drink worse whiskey than he used to drink when he was single."

AFTERWORD

Harry never fully recovered from his stroke. Although he could read some words on a map of the United States, he was unable to write again. He regained some speech but most of the words came out incorrectly. He would say "scott" when he meant "coat," "ray" when he meant "rain," "yarb" for "yard." He learned to pantomime for his failed speech, for example raising an imaginary glass to his lips when he could not say the word *drink*. Harry died in his sleep on January 19, 1956, shortly after listening to a broadcast of *Die Meistersinger* on the radio. His body was displayed in a little funeral home less than a block from his home. There were no services. His remains were taken to Loudon Park Cemetery, where they were cremated and the ashes placed next to his wife Sarah in the family plot. Harry's home at 1524 Hollins Street has been given museum status and is open to the public Wednesdays through Sundays.

August passed away in May 1967 after a life devoted to caring for his older brother.

Siegfried Weisberger died in March 1984 at the age of eighty-eight in Cambridge, Maryland. The last words he uttered were, "The Age of the Boob is upon us."

Howard never married. He succumbed to a stroke during retirement at the Cross Winds Hotel in Miami Beach. When the apoplexy hit, he was not sitting in the same deck chair in which his father had died.

Jacob Bluestein developed gangrene in his remaining leg. Despite a second amputation, the disease spread into his thigh. He passed away at the Veterans Hospital in Brooklyn in 1954. While he was dying in the hospital, junkies broke into his apartment on St. Marks Place and stole his Crosley TV.

Wolfgang Gottesman drowned in 1952 when he was caught in the undertow while swimming on the beach in Asbury Park. At the time of his death, he and his wife were running a small postcard and souvenir shop on the boardwalk.

A fire destroyed Irwin Mandelblatt's bookshop.

Ann Elkin began work on a new novel whose heroine was a young woman who sailed with Columbus on his first expedition to the New World. The novel was never completed. She married a man who owned a chain of three dry-cleaning shops on the West Side. She went on welfare after her divorce.

Edgar Ardery left Macmillan to form his own publishing house, which later received protection under the Federal bankruptcy laws.

Mildred Hawksmith retired from the New York Public Library system in 1949. Although senile, she lived happily in a nursing home in North Fort Myers, Florida, using a walker to get to the dining hall, until her death in 1962.

Professor Homer Svalgard was dismissed from Columbia University following a peer-review investigation of plagiarism involving a paper on the French Revolution that contained unsubstantiated statements by a William Trevor Coxe.

Detective Sergeant Mulvey was promoted to lieutenant but six months later was busted to patrolman after an episode involving a sixteen-year-old girl that was never officially explained.

Richard James Larch served ten years in prison, after which he entered the ministry.

Ronald Newberry and Roberta Kelly were executed on February 26, 1950, in Ossining, New York.

Moise Klein sold his Fourth Avenue properties and later joined a consortium that built a luxury hotel with a ten-story atrium in the Times Square area.

Butterman's Funeral Home on Amsterdam Avenue is currently a nightclub called "The Improv," which features up-and-coming young comedians.

Pennsylvania Station is buried beneath a sterile complex of office towers and a loathsome athletic hall known as Madison Square Garden.

Chirpy escaped through an open window and was last seen in the company of a flock of pigeons flying south on The Bowery.

Brummell vanished after a careless letter carrier forgot to shut the front door on the way out.

Eighty and a half Fourth Avenue became a Mexican restaurant, the interior walls altered to white stucco and decorated with serapes.

There are no secondhand bookstores remaining on Fourth Avenue.

ABOUT THE AUTHOR

DON SWAIM was born in Wichita, Kansas; raised in Houston, Texas, and Pittsburgh, Pennsylvania; and educated at Ohio University in Athens. He was a news editor and reporter at the CBS-TV affiliate in Baltimore before joining WCBS in New York as an editor, producer, and writer. His broadcast about books and writers, "Book Beat," is heard on major radio stations through the CBS Radio Stations News Service.